SNOWBALL,
DRAGONFLY,
JEW

SELECTED TITLES BY STUART ROSS

I Have Come to Talk about Manners (Apt. 9 Press)
Buying Cigarettes for the Dog (Freehand Books)
Dead Cars in Managua (DC Books)
I Cut My Finger (Anvil Press)
Confessions of a Small Press Racketeer (Anvil Press)
Hey, Crumbling Balcony! Poems New & Selected (ECW Press)
Razovsky at Peace (ECW Press)
Farmer Gloomy's New Hybrid (ECW Press)
Henry Kafka & Other Stories (The Mercury Press)
The Inspiration Cha-Cha (ECW Press)
The Mud Game (w/ Gary Barwin; The Mercury Press)
The Pig Sleeps (w/ Mark Laba; Contra Mundo Books)
Wooden Rooster (Proper Tales Press)

ANTHOLOGIES

A Trip Around McFadden: A 70th Birthday Festschrift (w/ Jim
    Smith; Front Press/Proper Tales Press)
*Rogue Stimulus: The Stephen Harper Holiday Anthology for a
    Prorogued Parliament* (w/ Stephen Brockwell; Mansfield Press)
My Lump in the Bed: Love Poems for George W. Bush (Proper
    Tales Press)
Surreal Estate: 13 Canadian Poets Under the Influence (The
    Mercury Press)

SNOWBALL, DRAGONFLY, JEW

experiences;
define identity-
conveying heritage
sense of loss

Stuart Ross

snowball- mother's first
experience w/
Anti semitism-
violence. multi
generational

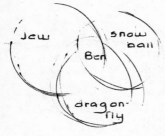

Jew / snow ball / Ben / dragon-fly

dragonfly- childhood/
memory- only
thing that influence
directly. all the
bug references. shaping
identity

MISFIT

ECW Press

Published by ECW Press
2120 Queen Street East, Suite 200, Toronto, Ontario, Canada M4E 1E2
416-694-3348 / info@ecwpress.com

LIBRARY AND ARCHIVES CANADA CATALOGUING IN PUBLICATION

Ross, Stuart
Snowball, dragonfly, Jew / Stuart Ross.

"A misFit book."
ISBN 978-1-77041-013-8
ALSO ISSUED AS: 978-1-55490-920-9 (PDF); 978-1-55490-983-4 (EPUB)

I. Title.

PS8585.O841S66 2011   C813'.54   C2010-907134-4

Developing Editor: Michael Holmes / a misFit book
Author Photo: Sydney Ross
Text Design: Tania Craan
Printing: Webcom 1 2 3 4 5

MIX
Paper from
responsible sources
FSC® C004071

The publication of *Snowball, Dragonfly, Jew* has been generously supported
by the Canada Council for the Arts, which last year invested $20.1 million in writing
and publishing throughout Canada, by the Ontario Arts Council, by the Government
of Ontario through Ontario Book Publishing Tax Credit, by the OMDC Book Fund, an
initiative of the Ontario Media Development Corporation, and by the Government of
Canada through the Canada Book Fund.

Canada Council Conseil des Arts
for the Arts   du Canada

Canadä

ONTARIO ARTS COUNCIL
CONSEIL DES ARTS DE L'ONTARIO

PRINTED AND BOUND IN CANADA

In memory of Shirley Ross

plot
- chapters were reorganized, not planned
- takes place in childhood 8-12, in between
  [death of mom - dad, university years, after
    his father's death
  ↳ and / performing period
- WWI and WWII - haunt him about Judaism

Themes
- bugs?   - mental illness

- death (murder) p32   - family

- memory   - self-discovery

- small pleasures   - growing up

- role of art

- anti-Semitism

- war

- religion

Ralf = Urtz Zerndal (spelling)
       ↳ author of the Hitler we loved and why
         didn't want the reference, or he would have
         kept the name

Wrote it as a novel, not an autobiography-
distance was freeing

CONTENTS

THE
DREAM

To its surprise, the bullet sailed out of the gun my mother clutched unsteadily in both hands, and a moment later the big man's yellow hard hat leapt from his thick head, into the air.

When the hard hat had reached the exact height of the roof of Faggot's Hardware, it stopped. Its dull curve had been ruptured by a singed bullet hole just an inch from a jagged black insignia. It remained suspended far above our heads, and above the body of the big man who had slammed heavily to the sidewalk, like a piano falling ten floors.

We gazed up at the hard hat, then down at the man, then back up at the hard hat. From behind the plate-glass window of the hardware store, a stubby guy with a withered left arm and bushy black eyebrows gazed with us. A pencil poked out from behind his ear. I wondered if he was the same guy with a pencil behind his ear from when I was a kid.

My mother slowly lowered her hands, chewing on her bottom lip, as if she were thinking really hard. Then she carefully placed the gun in the paper Dominion grocery bag by her feet, among the cartons of milk, the bananas, the celery, the cornflakes, the little boxes of powdered Jell-O, the packet of dry farfel, the length of Chicago 59 salami, and the kosher steaks wrapped in leaking brown paper. We had Worcestershire sauce in the fridge at home.

I glanced at my big brother, Jake. He was squinting quietly, in thought. His hand rested lightly on my shoulder. More people, some of them our neighbours, began to emerge from the shops to see what had happened. Toots Rosen, Marky Adler, Frieda Laba, the father from the Nefskys — Wallace, was it? Walter? — they stepped out of the shoe store, the cigar store, the Liquor Control Board of Ontario, and the bank. They stepped out of the Red Ruby Chinese Restaurant. Across the street, in the park with the slides, the teeter-totter, and the incredible rocket-ship monkey bars, a few kids had run right up to the frost fence. Their noses poked through. Their hands were like claws on the criss-crossed metal.

On the sidewalk, the man neither spoke nor twitched. The shadow of a breeze rippled his thinning hair. His eyes were gently shut, a trickle of black blood leaking neatly from his blue temple. He lay motionless there, in front of the hardware store in Bathurst Manor Plaza, dreaming of a white, white world.

3

GEORGE CHUVALO'S SIGNATURE

I didn't mind ants or cotton boll weevils, and I sure didn't mind worms, undulating on hooks or sliding through moist soil, but anything with long and spindly legs scared the hell out of me: especially spiders, centipedes, and those really big mosquitoes that looked like they could lift a station wagon with their suction feet.

My friends and I were playing in the lake, floating around in our red, green, and blue rubber doughnuts, our butts hanging down through the holes into the cool water. We were splashing each other and debating who was better from *Man from U.N.C.L.E.* — Ira liked Napoleon Solo, because he always ended up with a girl, one with red lipstick and piled-up blond hair, but Sammy saw that as a weakness and argued that Illya Kuryakin was way cooler: he was immune to girls and had a Russian accent. I tried to make a case for Maxwell Smart, but he was only a half-hour long, like Captain Nice and Mr. Terrific, so he didn't even count. As Sammy puckered up and made kissing noises into the air, mocking Napoleon Solo, my eyes caught a glint of purple, a lightning flash of black, and I saw that a giant dragonfly had perched on my knee. Its wingspan was that of a crow, and its body was made of a thousand horrible segments, a thousand thoraxes, a thousand anthraxes, each sprouting a terrible hairy leg. Its pointy metallic head jerked from side to side, its jaws clanging open and shut like an assembly-line contraption that crushes things flat, and its blank black eyes drilled right into me.

First Ira screamed, and then I screamed. I began to kick my little pink legs, my butt slipping deeper into the water, but the metal creature just wouldn't let go. I could feel its needle feet gripping my knee, clinging stubbornly as my heart banged and my limbs thrashed, and the rubber float that held me on the surface of the water rocked like a ship in a storm.

5

Then I saw my bare feet swoop into the clouds, my toes poking right into them, and everything got loud, and thick, and echoey, and slow-motion. Water punched up into my nostrils, and my eyes went blurry with brine.

That thing of knowing how to swim, I hadn't bothered with it yet, though I could dog-paddle, I could just about dog-paddle. Luckily, we were close to the shore, and when my feet found the gritty bottom — the moss, the stones, the warm sand shifting between my toes — I pushed myself straight, and the water came only to my shoulders. My whole body shuddered, and I slid my hands down to my knees, plunging my face again into the water. I swiped spastically at my legs, grabbing for the winged monster.

But somehow, in all the chaos, it had disappeared, just pulled up its spiny pincer feet and winged away, hitching a ride across the lake with the warm breeze, engorged with my blood and maybe even some of my brain, I really didn't know for sure.

When I straightened again and pulled my head from the water, I was coughing, and Ira was laughing, bobbing around in his squeaking doughnut, and Sammy was laughing, too. They were cracking up, spluttering water all over the place. On the dock just a few metres away, Michelle was pointing and howling, and Naomi. They wore colourful two-piece swimsuits — the colour of dragonflies, in fact — and they laughed at me, these little girls with straight dark hair and dark eyes, because I had looked like I'd gone nuts. I had looked like something out of an Abbott and Costello movie you saw on TV on a Sunday afternoon, if your dad and brother weren't watching football, like that one when Costello got chased up the old church bell tower by a lumbering mummy.

That night, after we barbecued hot dogs for dinner, toasted some buns on the grill, and opened a can of Jolly Green Giant corn niblets, ho ho ho, we gathered around the boxing ring that had been set up in a clearing at the edge of the woods, not far from the beach. I noted that although it was called a boxing ring, it was square, and I imagined what it would be like if people wore square rings on their fingers. Or what if their fingers were actually square?

My brother had one hand on my shoulder, and he pointed up at the ring and said, "That guy's George Chuvalo!" A big white man with watery red eyes, a flop of thick, sweaty hair, and a nose both puffy and flat was dancing around on the mat, springing on the soles of his feet, throwing his gloved fists at the enormous open palms of a thin black man who wore a pressed white shirt and a straw boater. I pushed forward and gripped the edge of the platform, peering up between the ropes at the two dancing men. I watched their feet and their hands, and I watched their faces all tensed up and concentrating. George Chuvalo had thick, knotted shoulders and a chest that was puffed up like his internal organs were all going to burst through.

We heard the *smack smack smack* of glove against flesh, the sharp grunts, the rhythmic tapping of the boxer's feet against the mat. Everyone from our cluster of cottages was there, and from the cottages around the other side of the lake as well, whooping and cheering for George Chuvalo. His name made me think of "marshmallow," that's what it sounded like, so I thought of him as George Marshmallow, and I looked forward to nightfall, when we'd gather around the fire and roast marshmallows on the ends of sticks we found in the woods. I liked when my marshmallow caught fire and I blew it out, then tasted its charcoal shell before getting to the sweet, sticky ooze. My mom always said I'd burn my tongue and I should wait till the marshmallow cooled off, but I never did, because you had to eat it right away to get the full effect.

On the far side of the ring, nailed to a tree, was a big corrugated-cardboard sign in crooked handwriting:

George Chuvalo
Cottage Country Training Camp —
Welcome to Wapaska, George!

I asked my brother if George was staying in one of the cottages, but Jake said no, he was just visiting here, because his trainer, the skinny black man, had a cottage down the highway. George was going to be the heavyweight champion of the world, my brother told me, and I should go and find something to get his autograph on after the training demonstration.

I picked through the forest of legs, burst free, then ran towards the cottage we rented for two weeks every summer. I was going to get the autograph of George Marshmallow, the famous boxer, the future heavyweight champion of earth. I'd never seen a boxer before, never seen their glistening, puffy faces. And maybe I'd get the autograph of the skinny black man, too. I'd never seen a black man before.

UP AGAIN,
INTO THE
BELL TOWER

At university, I did only the minimum required to get by, and sometimes even less. All my profs knew it, knew how lazy I was, that I wasn't trying, that I had brains I wasn't putting to use. What I mainly stayed in university for were the interventions I enjoyed perpetrating, and when I wasn't perpetrating interventions, I was scheming to perpetrate them. Actually, I didn't know these acts as interventions then, because interventions were still only things the CIA did in Latin America, like mining harbours in Nicaragua, invading Panama and Grenada, and assassinating populist Guatemalan presidents. The things I did, I saw as absurdist guerrilla art happenings.

For example, I ran a campaign to get the dead Dada poet and performer Hugo Ball elected student-council president, and a guy I knew who was involved in counting the ballots told me we'd got more votes than the goof in a suit from the business faculty who was reported to have won. In 1916, in Zurich, Hugo Ball and Emmy Hennings started up the Cabaret Voltaire, a home for artists, writers, and musicians. For one notorious performance, Ball wore a suit made primarily of cardboard tubes and cardboard wings. He droned non-existent words, and would someday become — if it weren't for a cover-up — the student president of a large Canadian university.

Another time, I sent terrorist letters to the campus newspaper. I threatened to spit into the open vats of ketchup, relish, and mustard in the student-building cafeteria if they didn't cover them up and install pump dispensers. It really bugged me when I lined up for ketchup for my turkey steakette only to find the ketchup tub swimming with plastic spoons, crumpled serviettes, speckles of mustard and relish, and maybe a pack of matches from the strip club, Shaky's, across the road. Then I began another letter campaign claiming I was chipping one square inch every day from the huge, blobby Henry Moore sculpture in the foyer of the administration complex — they posted guards there for a few weeks and frisked anyone who didn't work in the offices. I signed my letters "James Osterberg," which was Iggy Pop's real name. My favourite Iggy Pop song was "The Passenger."

These interventions, plus the occasional girlfriend who couldn't get anyone better, were what kept me on campus, if not actually in lecture halls or biology labs. ("Stop the Nazi Delousing of Locusts!" was another of my happenings after I had to gas a live locust in a compulsory science class.) The truth was, I couldn't concentrate on anything in university, because I didn't care, so it made no difference whether or not I attended classes.

So I was cutting my politics seminar again — something about Herbert Marcuse, or maybe Herbert Hoover — and sitting a few rows from the back in the rep cinema on College Street. James Stewart was dragging Kim Novak up the steep, winding stone steps of a church tower. It was excruciating; it had never taken this long before. I hoped

13

that somehow this time it would turn out differently. Stewart would come to his senses, slump onto the steps and weep, pleading for forgiveness. Novak, tears glistening in her glorious dark eyes, would crouch down and comfort him, then kiss his eyelids, and his forehead, and his cheeks, and his lips, and she and Stewart would walk slowly down the narrow spiral staircase again, holding each other for support.

But, just as they had the last time, and the time before that, they reached the top of the tower, sweat glistening on James Stewart's clenched brow, sadness and terror waltzing in Kim Novak's eyes. And then the nun appeared out of nowhere — the nun always appears out of nowhere, always — and the bell clanged like thunder. And then a startled Kim Novak stumbled backwards a few steps, just one step too many, and flailed silently out the window, leaving behind only the resounding absence of Kim Novak.

So it was that I wound up weeping, just as I always had when I watched this film. I wept at the end, but I also wept at that part where James Stewart says to Kim Novak, "Your hair . . ." as, fastening a locket around her smooth pale neck from behind, he transforms her into his dead lover, even though he actually has no dead lover, the whole thing's been faked, he's been duped.

And as the credits began rolling up the screen, the familiar strains of Bernard Herrmann's mournful "*Vertigo* Theme" welling again, to haunt me forever, I heard shouting behind me. I turned and saw two men, a couple of rows down, lunge for each other, swinging their fists. Their girlfriends struggled to hold them back, and then *they* began shouting, too, begging the men to stop, to just leave, to forget about it, to just forget the whole thing.

15

One guy had been whispering loudly to his girlfriend throughout the movie — even the part where James Stewart said to Kim Novak, "Your hair . . ." — and the other guy had been hissing at him to shut the fuck up, there was a movie on. And now they were going to kill each other, right here in this rep cinema on College Street.

The credits for one of the greatest works of Western art were rolling up the screen, and these two guys were going to rip each other's throats out.

I pulled myself to my feet and sidled along my row into the aisle. I felt tired and leaden. I was despondent. As I walked towards the red exit sign, I heard thuds behind me, fists on chests and maybe jaws, and then screams. I looked down at my hand and saw that I was still clenching an empty soft-drink container. It was crumpled in my fist. I felt cold, sticky syrup between my fingers.

Out on the sidewalk, it was raining just enough to be called rain. A sunny, hot afternoon had turned into something dark, wet, and chilly while James Stewart had been trying to bring a dead woman back to life. Wear this, he said. Now wear this, now put this around your neck, that's it, and put your hair up, yes, like this. . . .

The warped wooden display tables outside the men's shoe stores along College Street were covered in clear plastic sheets, rain running in small rivulets along the folds. I ran my fingertips over the plastic as I walked on legs that felt like tree trunks. I peered through the window of Sherman Tailors. A small man with white hair and smiling eyes was folding dress pants, stacking them up on a table. Another table featured a disorganized heap of bargain *schmatas*. My mother used to look at what I was wearing and say, "You're going to school in those *schmatas*?"

A couple of blocks from the cinema, I slipped into a doughnut shop and asked for a black coffee. It was bright in there, the air buzzing with the hum of the coffee maker, the ticking of the clock, and the rustle of newspapers. In the far corner, beside a big plant, a bearded man in a turban was pounding on the side of a payphone — he looked like he'd been doing it for hours. My head was throbbing, and my legs were unsteady. I fell into a moulded plastic chair at the long, winding counter and sipped at my cup, letting my eyelids slide shut.

When I open my eyes, I thought, Kim Novak will be sitting in the seat next to mine. She'll wear a grey dress and matching jacket, her smooth pale flesh visible in the vee of her collar. She'll say, in that soft, deep voice of hers, always so tentative, as if she's wondering whether she's pronouncing her words correctly, "Don't worry, Ben, I'm alive. I didn't fall. I lead a quiet life now, and raise llamas on my ranch, and take long walks with my veterinarian husband, away from the cameras and the

17

bullying directors and the gossip columnists and the endless steps leading up into dark church towers."

And then she reaches out a slender hand and says, "Your hair . . ."

I take a few steps back towards the window, and Kim Novak breaks into a huge smile. "I'm just kidding, Ben. Let me get you another coffee."

On the sidewalk outside, a nun walks by.

THE PLASTIC CONTAINER, EMPTY

My mother wouldn't let me bring my catfish into the cottage. I kept it in a plastic ice-cream container that I'd filled with water. First it had held spumoni ice cream, which was my dad's favourite, even though no one could tell me what spumoni was. Then the container had held wooden clothes pegs, which my mother used to clip up our laundry on the clothesline, but I'd dumped these out into a paper bag.

You could use a plastic ice-cream container for just about anything. It could hold things, or be a Turkish guy's hat, or you could melt it with a pack of matches and make it smell everything up, or you could just kick it into the grass. Also, bullets would bounce right off it.

I carried my catfish in the ice-cream container out onto the wooden porch and balanced it on the railing, then peered down into it and watched the pink-grey fish swim silently in tight little circles, its whiskers trailing along on either side of its head. That's what made it like a cat — the silence and the whiskers. Also because it was called a "catfish."

Night was just beginning to fall, and the air was damp, so the mosquitoes were biting like crazy. I scratched at the little white bumps they left on my flesh until I started to bleed. From across the clearing, where the biggest cottage stood, came the sound of ragtime music from the Borensteins' player piano. Someone was in there, pumping away at the pedals, and someone else was in there shouting. There was always shouting coming from the Borensteins' enormous cottage, the biggest in Wapaska. Al Borenstein and Bill Borenstein were at each other's throats over who owned the pier. They were brothers, like Jake and me, and I didn't understand why they couldn't just share the pier. There was plenty of room for everybody on the pier, for people and for spiders, and you could tie boats to it, and jump off it into the water, and fish from it if you wanted.

So there was the music of the Borensteins' player piano, and there was the shouting, and there was the silent swish of my catfish circling in its new home, wondering what spumoni is, and there was the smell of macaroni frying up on the stove wafting out through the screen door behind me.

My mother fried my macaroni because I didn't like it mushy the way the rest of my family liked it, all orange and creamy with milk. My mother always had to do something different with my food or else I wouldn't eat it. I didn't want to cause her aggravation, but I didn't like my macaroni all mushy; I didn't like my peanut-butter sandwich with jam, which reminded me of blood; I didn't like tomato pieces in my vegetable soup, or even tomato seeds floating on the surface, because it reminded me of guts; I didn't like my Coca-Cola served in a green glass, because green meant snot; I didn't like any bones attached to the meat in my stew, because that was like eating an animal; I didn't like milk in my cereal, which was usually

21

Lucky Charms, because it made me gag, the way it got so soggy.

After you prepared macaroni using the normal method, you could fry it. That way, it turned golden-brown and had crunchy bits in it, which I liked best. My mother would spend about half an hour scouring the frying pan afterward with hot water and an SOS pad, but first I'd scrape off all the leftover crunchy bits with a fork, and eat those, too.

[The catfish swam around and around in the plastic ice-cream container. The universe of the ice-cream container wasn't as big as the lake we'd got the catfish out of, but I figured it was still a pretty good environment. In the ice-cream container, the catfish didn't have to make as many decisions. I poked a fingertip into the cool water and felt the fish brush against me. When I pulled my finger out again, it had catfish water on it. If I didn't wash that off soon with soap and normal water, it'd eat my flesh right down to the bone. Catfish water was like acid, just like a cat's tongue. I sat down on the top step of the porch and listened to the rag-time music and the Borenstein brothers fighting. I listened to the crickets chirping, a sound Jake

22

acid - fun joke or anxiety?

small bucket = simple life, beauty in every day things

told me they made with their legs, not with their mouths. I sucked the bitter catfish water from my finger. Up the hill towards the rich cottages, the sun was an orange ball. It was one of those days when you could tell it was three-dimensional. I got up, pushed through the screen door, sat down at the table with Jake, Mom, and Dad, and ate my fried macaroni off a metal plate with a scene from *The Cat in the Hat*.]

In the morning, I was the first to wake up. The thin curtains were flapping at the window, and there was the inexplicable but not unexpected smell of soap in the air. Every morning the air smelled like soap here at the cottages. It came wafting in through the window, as if somebody was cleaning something somewhere. I examined the ceiling for spiders, as I did every morning. If I saw one, I wouldn't leave my bed until Dad came into the room and killed it. I knew that if I moved, it would lower itself down from its web and get me.

Jake was lying on his back in the next bed, wheezing, his mouth hanging open. He had a boner like he did every morning. I hadn't even been awake when he'd come home. He liked to stay out late, playing with the girls out on the beach or in the rec centre where we sometimes had parties. I slipped out of my bed and felt the breeze from the open window hit the sweat that covered my body. I scratched at my mosquito bites as I peeled off my damp pyjamas and pulled on shorts and a *Jetsons* T-shirt. We didn't have TV at the cottage, and my *Jetsons* T-shirt was the closest I got to watching cartoons.

In the kitchen, I poured some orange juice from a glass jug into a blue metal glass and drank it in one gulp, then headed for the front door. I opened the door quietly and peered out. The ice-cream container was gone from the railing. Where it had sat last night there was nothing but peeling green paint. I rushed out and leaned over the side of the porch. The container lay on the dry dirt below, a dark stain at its open end. In the stain were tidy little footprints.

Somewhere under a cottage, or perhaps in the boathouse, or in a tunnel beneath one of the gentle grassy inclines, a raccoon had my catfish. He looked at it with his beady black eyes, turning it around and around in his leathery paws. The catfish shivered in fear, or perhaps because it was just so cold out of the water, out of the calm and beautiful world that was the plastic ice-cream container.

A GUY
IN A GUY'S
ARMS — intimacy permitted between men only in this situation

Beneath the red-carpeted lobby of the Place Bonaventure Hotel, monks glided silently as catfish through corridors lit only by candles set in the walls. When my mother and I took trips to Montreal, where she liked to visit antique shops and art galleries, I'd crouch at the top of the escalator and peer down to watch them. It was like an ant farm down there, monks streaming in every direction, their antennae wagging, black robes draped over their thoraxes. I didn't get why there were monks under the Place Bonaventure Hotel, unless the hotel was built on top of a monastery because the monastery hadn't wanted to move when the hotel people bought the land. Also it was interesting that the word *monk* fit into the word *monkey*, because there was something monkey-like about monks. Or maybe it was just because the words sounded the same that I thought that.

But also, I had a teacher at Hebrew school named Mr. Munk, though his name reminded me more of chipmunks than of monkeys. Munk was a strange name for a Hebrew teacher, I thought, because there wasn't anything much Jewish about monks. Mr. Munk was the kind of teacher who made you want to not go to Hebrew school, as if learning Hebrew wasn't itself already enough of a reason. He was tall and thin and pale, like a monk, and his thin lips never smiled. His thin eyebrows never smiled either. Even on the hottest days, he wore a tie knotted tight up into his throat. His tie also never smiled.

Once, when Sammy was turned around in his desk and whispering to me during class, whispering something about the previous night's episode of *The Time Tunnel*, where Doug and Tony ended up with their heads in guillotines during the French Revolution, Mr. Munk was suddenly looming over us. He grabbed Sammy's wrist and slammed a yardstick down on the back of his

27

hand, right across the knuckles. Maybe because I wasn't turned around, he didn't do the same to me. But for the rest of that class, everyone was silent as we learned the words *bayit*, *yeled*, and *yelda*. House, boy, and girl. *David is a boy. Esther is a girl. David and Esther live in a house.* We were all silent. We were all thinking that in two more years we'd have our bar mitzvahs, everyone would give us presents, like some money or maybe the *Junior Jewish Encyclopedia* in a slipcase, and Hebrew school would finally be behind us.

People spoke French in Montreal, but in the lobby of the Place Bonaventure Hotel they spoke all sorts of languages. We couldn't speak French, but we knew words like *oui* and *non*, and *casa* and *bayit*, and I could also say *Pitou! Pitou! Donnez-moi le poulet!* Pitou was a dog, and poulet was a chicken. But when the lady with black stockings who cleaned our room on the seventeenth floor came in, I tried to show her my Johnny Seven (with night-vision goggles). She didn't understand when I explained that it could kill people in seven different ways, which was why it was called the Johnny Seven, because it could kill people in seven different ways. I made stabbing motions with the bayonet, like I was stabbing a guy in the stomach, twisting the knife around between his ribs, and I unhooked the hand grenade and pretended to throw it, but she just smiled and made the beds. Her black stockings really stood out against the white bedsheets.

We'd been here once with my father, and he'd told me Aldo Ray was in the lobby. I looked over where he was pointing and saw a fat bald man in a suit standing by the check-in counter. I asked my father if Aldo Ray was one of the monks — he had a name like a monk, you could imagine a monk named Aldo Ray — but my father just laughed and lit up another cigarette. In those days you could smoke cigarettes in the lobby of the Place Bonaventure Hotel as you sat in the big cushiony chairs under the enormous crystal chandeliers.

"What monks?" he asked.

"The ones in the basement," I said, pointing towards the escalator.

"Monks in the basement!" My father laughed again and tapped the ash from his cigarette into a silver ashtray that stood on the red carpet, then took a deep drag and coughed a bit. "Aldo Ray is an actor — come on, you've seen him on TV. He was in *We're No Angels* with Humphrey Bogart, and a lot of war films. Aldo Ray. Remember Aldo Ray?"

I remembered *We're No Angels*. That was the one where these three guys escape from the prison on Devil's Island and they have a little snake named Adolf, as in Adolf Hitler. It was pretty funny. I thought of the fat guy and decided that must have been Aldo Ray. When I grew up and saw the movie again, on video, I was surprised to find out that the fat guy was Peter Ustinov, and Aldo Ray was the skinny guy. He was the skinny guy, but he'd gotten fat by the time he got to Montreal and checked in at the Place Bonaventure Hotel.

In war movies, everyone was skinny and everyone was unshaven. Their faces were smeared with dirt and sweat, and they shouted whenever they talked. A film of sweat covered their foreheads and ran along their upper lips. They lay limp in one another's arms when they died, and they always said a thing before they died, or at least half a thing, and that was the only time they didn't shout.

The guy who was okay would say to the guy who was dying, "You'll be fine, Mac. Everything's going to be okay." But you could see he was trembling because he didn't really believe what he was saying.

The guy who wasn't okay, who was in fact dying, would always laugh quietly, staring off into the distance, eyes focussed on nothing at all. "We really showed them, eh, Charlie?" the guy would say, and then he'd cough weakly, like he was smoking.

"Tell Margaret I'd already picked out the ring, Charlie, and I was going to . . ." he'd say, and then his head would fall softly to one side and the guy who was okay would say, "Mac! Mac!"

"Hey, Charlie, I hope you don't mind if I welsh on that fin I owe you," the guy would say.

"There's a letter for Margaret in my bag — make sure she gets it, will you?" the guy would say, and the other guy would say, "Yeah, of course, Mac, of course. I'll bring it to her myself."

"It's really dark, Charlie," the dying guy would say, and though his eyes would be open, you could tell he couldn't see anything. "How come it's so dark? Isn't it afternoon? I can't. . . ."

kind of a jolt back to reality, not romantic/ intimate

[These were simple deaths. There were no venti-lators, no monitors with jagged lines on them, no gurneys stacked with towels, no *beep-beep-beeps* or sudden shrill alarms. There was no continual din of the loudspeaker, no frantic footsteps rushing down the hallway, no rotating red lights, no metal *sneaky* beds too short for my father's long, thin legs.]

These deaths happened mainly outside, in a patch of bushes, in a ditch by a dirt road, in a rice field, or maybe in an empty shack where a family used to live before the war drove them out.

32   The guy lying in the other guy's arms would have a moist spot on his shirt where the bullet went into him. It was always in black-and-white, because war was in black-and-white, and also because we didn't have a colour TV, and the moist spot would be almost black. Sometimes the guy lying in the other guy's arms would have an arrow sticking out of him, but that was a different kind of war.

Sometimes you wouldn't see any kind of wound at all, and it was like the guy died just because he was too tired to keep fighting [I didn't realize then that that was why most people died.] *true life*

war is in black and white—thing of the past. who's good, who's bad?

THE SACREDNESS
OF BOOKS, AND
ALSO A BIG BOY

An ant kept crawling up my bare leg, and I kept brushing it off. I'd barely finish reading a page, and then I'd feel the tickle on my calf again. It was a black ant. It was ant feet on my calf. This park was filled with ants.

The book was *Black Like Me*, by John Howard Griffin, which was maybe a weird thing for a fourteen-year-old white boy to be reading. John Howard Griffin was a white American man who painted his face black so he could see what it was like to be a black man in the United States. I had only ever seen a few black people, because there weren't a lot of black people in Bathurst Manor, and only two at my school, but after Martin Luther King was assassinated by James Earl Ray, and Sammy wrote his essay "Martin Luther Was a Very Good King," which everyone in class clapped for, I started seeing them everywhere. Then I found this book on my mother's bookshelf, crammed between the Chaim Potok paperbacks and the Harold Robbins paperbacks, all of which I'd combed thoroughly for the words *breast*, *nipple*, *caress*, *buttock*, and *creamy*. None of those words had so far showed up in *Black Like Me*, but I liked the book anyway.

Just as I was glancing down at my calf to brush off the black ant — or perhaps it was a different black ant, the first one having said, *Man, I can't get up there, why don't you give it a try?* — I noticed a pair of big blue running shoes come to a stop right in front of me. I looked up and there was a big kid with short black hair who I sometimes saw in the schoolyard and sometimes out in front of the cigar store at Bathurst Manor Plaza with a bunch of other kids.

"Hey, why'd you beat up my brother?" he said. He had a small bubble of snot in his right nostril. He wore a red baseball cap that I thought at first said "North York Bagels," but then I realized it was "North York Beagles." His hands were dirty and he hadn't cut his fingernails in about thirty years, even though he was probably only sixteen.

I closed my book on my index finger, keeping the page. I didn't say anything to him, but I could feel my heart pounding in my chest.

"Why'd you beat up my little brother — my little brother says you really beat him up. And also you kicked him, too."

"I don't even know your little brother," I told the big boy, even though I didn't know for sure, because I didn't know who his little brother was. "I never beat anyone up."

He drew the back of his left hand across his nose, smearing the snot bubble across his upper lip like a moustache. He was almost old enough to shave, one of those kids old enough to shave. Soon he'd have little bits of toilet paper stuck all over his face like my dad.

"I don't like when a Jew picks on my brother," he said. "I don't like when a Jew does *anything*."

The Jew thing changed everything.

When you said "Jew," that meant you didn't like the person. But if you said "Jewish person," everything was okay. For example, you would throw a snowball at someone and say, "You're a Jew!" But if you said, "You are a Jewish person," you probably wouldn't be throwing a snowball at someone.

When my mother walked to school in the 1930s, other kids pelted her with snowballs and called her a Jew. My mother was four years old, and she didn't even speak English back then. She spoke Yiddish, and her older sisters tried to shut her up, tried to make her stop talking in public until she could speak English.

"Look, man," I said, getting up and reaching for the little knapsack at my feet, "I didn't beat anyone up. I don't know what you're talking about."

"Yeah, right. What's that book you got there, Jew-boy?"

My mother used to tell me that it was okay to be friends with gentiles, a word I always associated with "gentle," but that if it really came down to it, the only people we could trust were other Jews. My friends were named Sidney, Murray, Harvey, Elliott, Sammy, and Ira, but there was a Peter and a Chris, as well. Under certain social, economic, and political conditions, Peter and Chris would turn on me in a second, stab me in the back, throw

me in a gas chamber, and turn my fat into cand
wax and my hair into a wig. At least, that's what
my mother said.

This boy, this very big boy, had straight black
hair and olive skin. He was Italian. He was the
grandson of Benito Mussolini, whose name had
"Moose" in it, and Moose was a character from
the *Archie* comics. I'd never had an Italian friend.
They were really good at sports and they talked
with a kind of accent. There was one Italian kid in
our school named Mario, who was
but was also tied with Sidney for
Wilmington Junior High. He had dark eyes and
long eyelashes and blond hair and thick lips. He
wore shirts without sleeves, but still he did really
well in science. He could light a Bunsen burner in
a second and recite the memory thing about plants:
*Up the xylem, down the phloem, that's the way the
foodstuffs roam.* Mr. Joshua, the science teacher,
liked him probably better than any other student.

"It's nothing," I said, about the book.

"You read books even when you're not at
school. What's the big idea? You trying to show
off, Jew-boy?" His hand darted out like a snake's

tongue and grabbed my wrist before I'd got the book into my knapsack.

"No," I said.

I knew that I should defend myself. The problem with the Jews in the Second World War, with my mother's aunts and uncles and her grandparents, was that they just marched along to the trains and didn't fight back. That's what my mother said. Same with me: I thought maybe I could just get out of this somehow, if I avoided escalating the confrontation. "Look, I'm sorry —"

"Wreck it," the big boy said.

"What?"

"Rip it in half." He let go of my wrist.

I looked down at the book in my hand, then I looked up at him. I was standing now, but I still had to look up to see his face. If I looked directly forward, I could see the collar of his white T-shirt, spotted with brown and green stains and shredded by chew marks.

"You want my sandwich?" I asked. "I've got a cheese sandwich. On challah."

"Rip it in half," he said again.

"No, you can have it all."

"The book. I'm talking about the book, wise guy."

I thought about snatching up my knapsack and making a run for it. He grabbed a handful of the curly hair on the back of my head, just like he'd read my mind. I remembered the photographs I'd seen of huge mountains of human hair in the concentration camps. I couldn't remember what they'd done with it, what they'd made with it, the Nazis, but I remembered that people with shaved heads all looked the same. You couldn't tell one from the other, so you had to put numbers on their arms or else you'd lose track of who was who.

My father didn't read much, except for the sports section of the newspaper and the occasional spy novel, but he respected me and my mom and Jake for reading a lot. It was like we were doing something mystical that he didn't completely understand. He'd always talk to us, though, while we were reading — *Do you want a wurst sandwich?* — because he figured wurst sandwiches were on the same level of importance as books, as mystical as books. *Want anything from the cigar store?*

I took a deep breath. Maybe if I just ripped *Black Like Me* in half, the big boy would let me go, let go of my hair. I clutched the first hundred pages in my left hand and the rest — another hundred pages or so — in my right. I tugged hard and steady, until the book split right down the binding and separated into two pieces.

There. I'd ripped a book in half.

I'd wrecked a book.

His fist tightened on my hair, yanking my head back a little. "Rip it some more."

Now was the time to fight back. On the other hand, the pages were numbered, like bald people's arms, and I'd still be able to read it, even though it wouldn't feel like a book anymore. It would be more like just a pile of pieces of paper. I could hold it together with an elastic band or maybe use some scotch tape on it.

I ripped each half several more times and shuffled the sections, so they'd be out of order. "Okay?" I said.

"Throw it in the garbage." With his free hand, he gestured to an overflowing garbage basket on the grass nearby. "Stuff it in there."

40

Now was the time to fight back. This was the deciding moment. I was going to be a Jew who fought back.

Later, after dark, I biked back to the garbage basket and rummaged through the potato-chip bags and the banana peels and the Canada Dry ginger ale cans. The book was gone. John Howard Griffin had dyed his face black and wandered through the American South, and dated black girls, and got threatened, and mistreated, and beat up.

Then he wrote a book about it, which I ripped up and stuffed in a garbage basket.

THEY TALKED
ABOUT ME

After my father had died, after he was completely dead, twenty-six years after he'd seen Aldo Ray, the skinny one now fat, in the lobby of the Place Bonaventure Hotel in Montreal, I wore his shirts during all my performances. During the shiva, I had gone through his closet and taken everything that fit me. Some of my mother's clothes were still there, and I took a few of her scarves. Someday I'd give them to someone, the scarves my mother had worn around her neck.

My mother had never seen my shows, I called them shows, but after she had died, after she was completely dead, my father started coming to all my openings. He had no idea what I was doing — he was sure it was supposed to mean something and he was a simple man, not about to absorb meaning — but he saw me win the approval of those who came to my shows, and this pleased him. He told me he liked to hear the people at my performances laugh, which they usually did, even if I hadn't meant them to.

I told him not to worry, that he wasn't missing anything, it's not like there was any great symbolism. I told him he should just sit back and enjoy, or sit back and get pissed off, or laugh, or weep, or whatever he wanted to do. I think he usually napped.

"Whatever response you have is the correct response," I told him. "It's not a matter of what I'm trying to say, but of what you get out of it. After all, everyone brings a different life experience to any piece of art."

"Well, I'm not an artist like your mother was — I don't know what this crazy kind of art you do is all about," he replied. "Just like you don't understand football or hockey."

So I devised a performance with him in mind, something he'd understand for sure, whatever "understand" meant. I called it "Night of a Thousand

Doughnuts," and I rented Billy Billy Donuts for the piece. Billy Billy was across the road from the hospital where my mother had died. My father and I had spent a lot of hours there, as we killed time and waited for Mom to come out of her coma, for her eyes to flicker or her finger to twitch, which we must have known, we must have known, was not in the cards.

As both the art crowd and the doughnut-shop crowd lined up along the counter to feed me doughnuts for "Night of a Thousand Doughnuts," to feed me raised chocolate, chocolate peanut, coconut, vanilla iced, cream-filled, double chocolate, honey-glazed, marble swirl, I kept an eye on the door, waiting for Dad to arrive. Every time I got a Hawaiian sprinkle, my father's favourite kind, I wanted to cry. Now my father is dead and he will never again bite into a Hawaiian sprinkle doughnut with his false teeth. He'd eat a doughnut, slurp down a black coffee, and smoke a Rothmans. Still, to this day, when I eat a Hawaiian sprinkle doughnut, I feel like crying. And sometimes I do cry.

He never showed up for "Night of a Thousand Doughnuts," but phoned the next morning in between my bouts of vomit and diarrhea. "How'd it go, your doughnut thing?" and he laughed a little, then made that sucking noise that meant he was smoking, even though he swore to me he'd quit. "I planned on coming, but Marsha didn't feel like it, so we went to see a funny movie instead. Marsha would have just thought you were doing crazy things anyway. She's not cultured like your mother was."

For my father, art meant Kirk Douglas as Vincent Van Gogh, Charlton Heston in *The Agony and the Ecstasy*, and maybe that Oldenburg hamburger in the Art Gallery of Ontario. So after my father died, I made him an unknowing, posthumous collaborator in my art.

For "Stagger," a piece that won me a lot of notoriety and a nomination for a prize named after a dead art patron that nobody liked, I wore one of the shirts I'd salvaged from my father's closet. It was a formal white shirt with thin red stripes at half-inch intervals. The collars buttoned down, and the sleeves ballooned out. I figured it would go nicely with a pair of black dress pants and suspenders.

"Stagger" lasted twenty-four hours and took place in the window of Porter + Haas, a gallery in an upscale, boutique-laden district of the city, a former hippie enclave called Yorkville my wealthy uncle Simon had helped develop in the late 1960s. I made up the window to look like a concentrated version of the living room from my childhood home: a small couch with a floral fabric, a couple of coffee tables, a desk, and a bridge table with four folding chairs around it and a heap of mah-jong tiles on top.

Every surface was cluttered: family photos, vases, a cold cup of coffee, bowls of peanuts and jujubes, a metronome, a couple of ashtrays, a lighter in the form of a pirate's pistol, some loose change, glass and crystal animal figurines. Many of these items actually did belong to my family, retrieved from my mother's little gift shop after her death, and the rest I'd picked up at thrift stores.

The soundtrack for my performance emanated from one of those record-players-in-a-case — in fact, it had been Jake's. It stood in the centre of the gallery floor: a green, fake-fabric box that opened up, with a speaker on either side of the platter. A stack of singles stood beside it, and gallery-goers could choose between "Seven Little Girls (Sitting in the Back Seat)," "The Times They Are A-Changin'," "Mrs. Brown, You've Got a Lovely Daughter," "Eve of Destruction," "Girls, Girls, Girls," and a dozen other pop hits from my youth. "Stagger" began at its opening, 7 p.m. on a Friday night in September. A few days earlier, planes had slammed into some tall buildings in Manhattan, a thing I wished my dad had lived to see, because it was so spectacular and so horrifying at the same time.

I was already blindfolded and standing in the floor-to-ceiling window, among the furniture and knick-knacks, when the gallery goers started to arrive. They clustered on the sidewalk in front of Porter + Haas, strangers and friends, maybe even a critic or two, talking loudly. I could hear what they were saying, but because I was blindfolded they must have decided I was deaf. They talked about me. I could hear them talking about me.

Brenda, the gallery's curator, rapped on the window from the sidewalk at exactly seven o'clock, as I'd requested, and the voices fell silent. I could hear only the occasional honk of car horns on the

47

narrow streets around the gallery. Then there was the momentary scratch of stylus on vinyl, as the stylus found a groove, and the opening chords of Barry McGuire's "Eve of Destruction." My blood was coagulatin'.

I let my knees go a little rubbery and took a small outward step with my left foot, letting my weight fall naturally. Then I stepped again clumsily with my right foot, and kept going, letting my body achieve its own awkward momentum. I bumped into what must have been the coffee table, and something crystal shattered on the floor. I stumbled away from the noise and nearly fell back onto the couch, but caught myself. This was it, then. I would be staggering around this gallery window, in a stylized replica of my childhood living room, for the next twenty-four hours. One of the challenges was to keep my stagger from turning into a dance. I had to block out the music.

After a few minutes, I heard some laughter from the sidewalk in front of me, and then the murmuring began again, and soon I heard the sound of heels on the gallery's hardwood floor, as everyone filed inside to grab wine and celery sticks. I heard someone uncorking bottles. I heard the crunch of the celery sticks. A sheer lace curtain separated me, on the storefront-window platform, from the inside of the gallery. It was set a few centimetres in on the platform, so I could feel it and catch myself if I was about to fall over onto the gallery floor.

By the next evening, I would be dizzy and exhausted, my bladder about to burst, my legs numb, my thinking dream-infested. Brenda would have fed me a few carrots and some whole wheat bread in the morning, but I'd be ravenous. I'd imagine I was as fat as Aldo Ray in the lobby of the Place Bonaventure Hotel in 1969. Monks would come up the escalator, bearing enormous platters of fish and fresh fruit, just for me. Then a chandelier in the lobby would come crashing to the floor, breaking the collarbone of a sixty-two-year-old bellhop.

A BULLET IN HIS SPINE

My mother turned on the motor of the blue Valiant station wagon for a couple of minutes to blast some heat into the car. We sat in the front seat, shivering and sweating in the bulk of our winter coats. It was late February, and everything was crispy, covered with ice. The sun was just falling, leaving us in shadows, and the car rocked slightly in a strong wind that skipped candy-bar wrappers across the plaza's parking lot and sent Dominion bags sailing through the air like seagulls.

"He's been in there for over an hour," my mother complained quietly, as if talking only to herself. "He's usually a lot quicker. He's usually ten minutes, maybe a quarter of an hour. What's he doing in there?"

"Maybe he's chatting with the owner or something," I said. "If he's always in there, they must know him. Maybe he's like family. Maybe they're talking about some kind of new T-square."

My mother cut the motor again, and the white clouds that had been puffing up outside my window disappeared. It was silent in the car for a few minutes. Other cars drifted back and forth in front of us, leaving the plaza or just arriving. Some skidded a little on the ice, but everyone was careful. These were the days when everyone was careful when they drove.

A tiny old woman with bright red lipstick, no nose, and an enormous hunch between her shoulders shuffled slowly by on the wide strip of sidewalk that ran in front of the stores. Her head was uncovered, and her sparse, curly hair was dyed black. She wore a thick black coat that came past her knees. Her calves were covered in black stockings that bunched up near the ankles, just above the white running shoes she wore. The woman's head was pushed forward and down, and when she turned briefly towards us, it was like being looked at by an inquisitive crow. I knew that she spoke in

51

a thick Eastern European accent, even though she wasn't Jewish.

I looked over at my mother. Her wavy hair was brown and red, and her nose was straight and not very big, but it was definitely a nose. My mother's eyes were dark, like mine, and her lips were thin with pale lipstick. In photos, like the ones on our wall where the whole family was, and all these old men and women in black-and-white posing beside chairs, and the colour ones on the coffee tables and end tables in little stand-up frames, her lips were always pursed, but in real life they were never pursed. Would she look like the old woman shuffling along the sidewalk when she reached her eighties? Would a bump grow between her shoulders, and would her nose disappear? Would she dye her hair black and speak in a thick Eastern European accent?

The woman carried a heavy shopping bag in each hand and moved slowly. Even if she lived just a block from this plaza, it would take her half an hour to get home. But she knew ice, and she knew how to walk on it. If a woman like that fell, she'd break her hip. They always did, always broke their hips, and then they caught pneumonia, and then they ended up in intensive care, and then their grandchildren played with plastic toys on the floor beside their beds, played with their Johnny Sevens and their Mr. Potato Heads, and then people placed their ears close to these old women's mouths, and then a machine made a long beep and people heaved sighs of relief.

"Why would a Jew talk to him?" my mother said. "They know what he stands for, they know that he hates us. And why would he shop in a store *owned* by a Jew? It doesn't make any sense, Ben." Her voice was quiet but angry. She turned the key again in the ignition, and the station wagon began vibrating, hot air blasting from the two plastic vents in the dashboard.

At that moment, Rolf Köber stepped out of Faggot's Hardware. My mother and I watched without a word. Under his left arm he carried a large box, and with his right hand he was pushing his wallet into his pants pocket. He wore a brown cap with mufflers over his ears and a bulky blue winter coat. He reached into his coat pocket and took out a pair of brown mittens, working one onto each hand as he walked.

53

Trailing Köber were two more men, one a tall, thin elderly guy with a blast of white hair and wire-rimmed glasses. He was laughing and bantering with a much younger man, barely more than a teenager. The young man was blond and handsome, like a pretty prizefighter, and he walked with a limp. Without even looking back, Köber called something over his shoulder, and his companions nodded their heads in agreement.

"He's a piece of shit," my mother said as the three men climbed into an old green pickup truck, crammed together in the cab — the blond at the steering wheel, then the old man, then Köber by the passenger window. "Look at him laughing. He doesn't deserve to laugh — he wants all of us dead. He deserves a bullet in his spine."

As the pickup headed for the north exit of the parking lot, my mother shifted our car into gear and we rolled out of our spot. At first I thought my mother was going to follow Rolf Köber, but then she turned towards the opposite exit.

I was going to argue that no one actually deserved to die, no matter how hate-filled they were, but I didn't think my mother wanted to hear that. Besides, I didn't like mentioning death to her. A week earlier, she'd been diagnosed with breast cancer. The last thing I wanted was to remind her about death, even though I knew that she probably thought of nothing *but* death. This trait of non-confrontation — I'd gotten it from my father.

My father said all the time that my mother was a witch, because she always knew what we were thinking. "I don't want him dead," she said to me, confirming Dad's theory. "I like the idea that he'd be paralyzed and never be able to do anything about his hatred. He'd just sit in a crappy wheelchair and seethe for the rest of his miserable life. His wife would have to feed him and change his underwear. She'd go somewhere else for sex, because he wouldn't be able to get his little Nazi prick up."

Again, I was going to argue, but I kept my mouth shut.

"On second thought," she said, and I knew this was probably about her four-hundred-and-twelfth thought on the topic, "dead might be better. I'd spit on his grave."

55

Our car glided along Wilmington, onto Over-
brook, Shaftesbury, Pannahill. I saw the corner
where Mike Gould had pinned my arms behind
my back and egged on Peter Van Veld to throw a
dart at me. Peter laughed and aimed, and laughed
and aimed, but he didn't throw the dart, and Mike
got bored.

"What do you want for dinner tonight, Ben?
Fried macaroni?"

THE CANCER CAME BACK,
THE VERY NEXT DAY

Six months after the screening of *Vertigo*, the angry shouts and the fistfight, six months after James Stewart chased Kim Novak up those bell-tower stairs, that interminable chase yet again — the hair, the necklace, the nun, the flailing in mid-air, the silent thud — I was still barely able to leave my living-room sofa, much less my living room. The phone rang, and I fumbled for it on the end table; I said hello; someone talked to me; soon we hung up, and a moment later I couldn't remember who it had been or what we'd talked about.

Every thought I had, and there wasn't a lot of variety, felt like a dead body sprawled across the pavement of my skull. I cursed myself in my head, and I cursed myself aloud, and I tugged at my hair, hoping the physical pain would distract me from that other pain. Occasionally a friend would drop by with pizza or beer, but I was a drag, and I tried to be a drag, and I dragged everything and everyone along with me.

But as suddenly as I fell into that dark place, I woke one morning to find that I'd emerged into daylight, like when the Incredible Shrinking Man climbed up a thread and out his basement window, onto his lawn, where the glorious blades of grass towered above his head like skyscrapers. My first thought was that it was good I hadn't killed myself, that I'd clung to a hope that I'd crawl out of the abyss. My second thought was that it could happen again. And it did.

Eighteen months after I watched my mother exhale for the last time, watched her gently blow out the candles, I realized I'd been on the sofa three times as long as the first bout, three times as long as Operation Vertigo.

Again, the phone would ring, and I would watch it ring. This time I would just watch it ring. I would see wriggly ring lines emanate from it like it was a cartoon phone, a *Flintstones* phone. I thought about stretching out my arm to pick it up, to say hi, to say what's doing? oh nothing much here, just watching TV, I mean working on a new performance, I call it "Sofa/Couch/Chesterfield/Divan" and it consists of me lying on a sofa in my living room not answering the phone.

I lay on the sofa, which was a little short for the length of my legs, and watched TV, stupid game shows and identical talk shows, bad teens being carted off to boot camps, those were my favourite, and then watching them return to the show the next day, although really a week had passed, and hugging their boot-camp drill sergeant and giving their grandmas back the $32 they had stolen from behind the breadbox or inside the cookie jar, a cookie jar shaped like a panda, and kissing their mothers and crying and saying they'd be good now, they weren't sluts anymore, they were good girls now, they'd never be a problem again, and most important, they wouldn't dress all sexy and they'd try to lose some weight.

While I watched these shows, I thought about Kim Novak plunging out the window of the church tower, and I thought about Rolf Köber's face

59

slamming into the sidewalk in front of Faggot's Hardware and James Stewart standing over him, saying, "Your hair . . ."

During those months in the depths of the sofa, I wondered over and over whether my mother had actually done it, had followed through with her plan, avenged the flurry of snowballs, the deaths of her aunts and uncles in Poland a half-century earlier.

Had I actually seen her pull that trigger?

Was it true that Rolf Köber's hard hat hovered high above the entrance to Faggot's Hardware for one entire week, before it plummeted back down to the sidewalk, landing in the exact spot its owner had lain until he was taken away on a stretcher, covered in a sheet from head to toe? You'd think there'd be a plaque marking the location of such an extraordinary event. Should I go to Bathurst Manor Plaza to see if there was a plaque?

I thought of phoning Jake, or my father, and asking, "Did Mom kill that Nazi? Did she ever really get that gun?"

But Jake, Jake would ask me our mother's name, and then he'd ask me my name, and then he'd ask me what a Nazi was. As for Dad, he'd been so quiet ever since my mother's death. Ever since I'd walked out of her room in the ICU and said, "It's all over now; it was really peaceful. I just read her some poems and she stopped breathing." If Mom had actually killed Rolf Köber, my father probably didn't want to be reminded of it. If Mom hadn't killed Rolf Köber, my father would have said that I was like Jake, that I was nuts. I was nuts and I needed to see a shrink.

Had Mom told anyone but me about her plan? We sat in Bagel, Comrade! at Bathurst and Eglinton and she sipped on her coffee and told me she was making inquiries. Did I know anything about guns? Where could she get one? What kind would be easiest to operate? She was trying to impress me — she liked being a mother who could shock. And, of course, I knew nothing about guns, and she knew that. I knew only my Johnny Seven, and the seven ways it offered to kill a man.

Since her cancer had come back — I hated when she mentioned her cancer and tried always to change the subject — she'd embraced her old scheme with a new vigour. After all, what did she have to lose? Why did this piece of Nazi fuckshit have the right to live longer than she did? If she was getting kicked off the surface of this planet, she'd take the prick with her.

She saved clippings about him, of which there were plenty, mainly because of his fight to stay in Canada, and she started to follow his movements. He lived not far from where I'd grown up, on a street with only six houses, and my mom swore she saw him at Faggot's Hardware more than once.

In the winter it snowed, and it was hard for Mom to go out then. When I came to visit, she told me about the snowballs, how they'd hurled snowballs at her, a girl just four years old. What were those snowballs thinking as they flew towards her little curly-haired Jewish head? Was this why their flakes had floated down from the sky like ashes?

MISSING
THINGS

When we were in Grade 6, me and Sidney and Ira
had a girl in our class named Hedy Berkovitz. She
always looked sad; therefore I liked her. I thought I
was in love with her, even — I thought she was the
girl for me, but I was only ten. She had a very oval
head, olive skin, bright dark eyes, and a pointed
chin. She had short black hair and thin dark lips.
Hedy looked like she had the head of an ant, a very
beautiful ant. All she was missing were antennae.

I don't remember how I got there exactly, but
once I stood in her bathtub, in the bathtub in the
apartment building she lived in, across the road
from the library. That's all I remember. Standing in
Hedy's bathtub, dark-eyed Hedy's green bathtub,
which had no water in it. I thought to myself, *I*

am standing in the bathtub of Hedy the Ant-Head. Hedy's mother had only one leg and one of her arms was cut off at the elbow. We called that being "born wrong." Hedy's mother was born wrong.

At home later, after Hedy and I had finished the school project we were working on together (yes, a history project about pygmies! — that's why I was there!), I told my mother I didn't like to look at people who were born wrong and I asked her why people ended up like that.

"The doctors don't really know why people are born wrong," my mother told me, as she fried up some macaroni and I sipped a big glass of milk through a straw, "but if God didn't want them that way, he wouldn't have made them like that. They are a tragedy, though, and you should always treat them just like everybody else. They haven't done anything wrong." She scraped the macaroni onto my *Lost in Space* plate. "And try not to stare, Ben."

That was the first time I'd heard the word *tragedy*. Hedy's mother was a tragedy, and if Hedy and I got married ever, I'd have to see her tragedy all the time. I didn't like the way that arm that stopped at the elbow looked, and I wondered how

Hedy could stand looking at it, but obviously she was born with her mother missing all those parts, so she was probably used to it.

"To Hedy, it's normal to have a mom with just one leg and one arm," Ira told me while we cut pictures of spaceships out of his dad's *Encyclopaedia Britannica*, a thing for which we would later get hell. His parents were friends with Hedy's parents, and they played bridge together every Friday night. "*I* like to look at it," he added.

When we went to synagogue, which was only very occasionally, like when someone was having a bar mitzvah or during the high holidays, we saw Hedy's mother there, with a white lace thing on her hair. Nobody paid any special extra attention to Hedy's mother, but she was so dressed up, with a long skirt and long sleeves on her shirt, that you couldn't see all the things she was missing.

A few years later, Hedy came to my bar mitzvah because my parents let me invite ten friends. At the lunch, I had to sit up at the head table with my mom and dad and Jake, plus my grandfather, and my friends all sat at a round table at the very back of the room. While Jake was making a speech about

65

me, about what it was like to be my brother, about the dumb and funny things I did, and everyone was laughing, I saw Sammy lean over towards Hedy Berkovitz and whisper something in her ear. I got scared that maybe he was telling her that I had a crush on her still, that the pygmy project was the highlight my childhood, and that I'd made up a song about her:

Hedy the Ant-Head is really neat,
Hedy the Ant-Head walks down the street,
When I see her six legs and her thorax,
I find it really hard to relax.

Then my mother came up to the microphone and said how proud she and my dad were of me, and how proud they were of Jake, and that we were following important traditions, traditions that went way back to the old bearded guys in the photos on our wall. Her voice was shaking a little, so she stopped for about a minute. Then she started listing all the grandparents and other relatives who were dead now, but who would be so proud, and then she talked about all the aunts and uncles that she'd never known because "they turned to smoke over Poland." There was sadness in her voice, but even more there was anger. The whole room fell quiet, even at the table where my friends were.

After the lunch was over, I walked Hedy out to the parking lot where she was going to be picked up. She lived only a few blocks away from the Beth Emeth, but she was wearing such fancy clothes that it was decided she had to get a lift. Her dad didn't want her wearing fancy clothes around the streets. I was wearing fancy clothes, too: a matching camel-colour jacket and pants, and a black tie with diagonal blue stripes. I felt almost like an adult, but not like the "man" I was supposed to be after singing all those Hebrew words I didn't understand.

The door to Hedy's parents' car opened, and Hedy's mom stepped out. She called "Mazel tov, Ben!" in my direction and I saw that she had a hand coming out from each of her sleeves. A new hand!

As I was trying to digest this, Hedy stepped close to me and pressed her lips against my cheek. Hedy's lips were cool and thin, and I felt her antennae brush against my ear. "Congratulations, Ben," she said. "Thanks for inviting me — it was fun!" She

67

turned and skipped the few steps to her mother, leaving me with a boner in my dress pants.

Hedy's mother reached out with her left hand to take Hedy's hand, and I could see that the right hand was pale and waxy, and stuck in a position like it was about to strangle someone.

FINGERPRINTS

I remember *touch*.

That is that thing where part of another person comes into contact with part of you. Part of me. Skin and skin meet, either fleetingly or for a sustained period. A microbe hops from the groove of a fingerprint to a crevice in a lower lip.

An example of touch is, my father puts me in a headlock and holds me like that, but he's only playing around. It's something we've seen on TV on Saturday afternoons with Haystack Calhoun, Whipper Billy Watson, the Fabulous Kangaroos, and the Love Brothers (Reginald and Hartford), some of our favourite wrestlers at Maple Leaf Gardens.

Another example is, my mother presses her lips against my cheek and makes a loud smacking sound. It's an exaggeration of a real kiss, the kind I would eventually have with some girls who were not my mother. Or sometimes I'm lying in bed with a fever and my mother places her cool palm across my forehead and says, "Let me feel your *kepalah*." I get to stay home from school, but there's nothing good on TV.

Another example is, my brother Jake wraps both his hands around one of my wrists, and twists hard in opposite directions, which he calls an "Indian wrist burn." Afterwards my wrist is red and it stings. This was a torture that Indians did to white men.

My uncle Ronnie shakes my hand when he comes in the door, and when the handshake is over, there's a little toy soldier in my palm. He's made of a deep green plastic. He's got a backpack on and he carries a Johnny Seven.

My friend Ira flicks a ladybug off my shoulder and we watch it fly away, drifting over the lawn on a breeze.

Rabbi Kelman slaps me lightly on the cheek the first time I recite my entire bar-mitzvah portion by memory without making a mistake. "What a mensch," he says.

My first girlfriend, Joanne, pushes her hand down the front of my pants.

My next girlfriend, Carol, pushes her hand down the front of my pants.

The old guy at the cigar store brushes his fingertips against my palm as he hands me my change when I buy a bag of barbecue potato chips that are kosher for Passover. The clock on the wall behind him has a picture of Golda Meir, who tells me it's 3:43 p.m.

My grandmother, the one I knew until she died, not the other one, the one who died when I was six months old, reaches for my face and I flinch. Her fingernails are bright red. With the side of her index finger, she wipes the lipstick from my cheek, from where she just kissed me.

My mother's fingers, so thin, clasp my forearm weakly, so I can barely detect her grip, and she looks into my eyes and tells me I better take care of my father, because he doesn't even know how to buy a fresh tomato or a head of lettuce for himself.

I'm certain there are other instances of touch in my life, but right now I can't think of them.

THE MANY USES OF YAHRZEIT GLASSES

My grandfather's teeth hung suspended in the cloudy water in the clear glass on the edge of his green bathroom pedestal sink: white teeth, pink gums, magnified. I examined them silently, then reached forward and tapped the side of the glass. The teeth bobbed, as if they were laughing, and I jumped back, then ran from the bathroom, up the stairs, and hid behind the wing chair.

When people get old, their teeth fall out of their mouths, my dad told me. And when their teeth fall out, it gets hard to eat corn on the cob.

I imagined my grandfather's upper teeth falling out of his mouth in one entire row, like a row of corn, complete with his gums. Just like they looked in the glass on the edge of his sink. And then, maybe a few years later, his lower teeth fell out. Each morning he glued them back in so he could eat, but by night, the glue had lost its sticky properties, because of all the spit in his mouth. My grandfather was always clearing his throat and spitting. At night, from upstairs in my bedroom, where I read *Sad Sack* comic books and *Plastic Man* under the covers with a flashlight, I could hear him make throat noises. I covered my ears with my hands.

The glass that my grandfather's teeth floated in had once held a *yahrzeit* candle, lit for his wife, my grandmother, whom I had never met. He had a list of what day in every year he had to light a *yahrzeit* candle for his wife. The list was taped to the large mirror that sat on the pine dresser in his room. When he lit the *yahrzeit* candle, I wasn't allowed to blow it out, I wasn't allowed to burn bits of paper in it, and I wasn't allowed to play with the melted wax afterward, like I could with the Chanukah candles.

We also drank from *yahrzeit* glasses, after Mom cleaned out the last bit of wax from them. I drank milk out of the glasses and Jake drank pop. I liked to drink my milk with a straw, so that I could blow bubbles and make that glugging noise that bugged my parents so much. The bubbles would quickly multiply, until my milk reached the very top of the glass. Then I could blow them out, or drink them, or pop them with my straw.

I once climbed up on a dining room chair I'd placed on the dining room table, and I hung my pyjama top from a chandelier, just because it was fun to climb up on things and to hang things from things, and my mother yelled at me. What happened was, my grandfather had walked into the dining room from the kitchen, after slicing up some cow's tongue for lunch, and he thought that I'd hanged myself. I was eight years old. My mother yelled at me that I scared him so much, that it was like I was hanging from the chandelier, but then she hugged me, shaking her head the whole time.

People who eat cow's tongue were in jail in Poland during the First World War, because there's no other explanation for how you could come to eat cow's tongue. They were jailed by their own army because they didn't want to fight and they ran away just enough so that they'd be captured. In jail, the soldiers who were guarding them ate all the good parts of the cow, like the steaks and the spare ribs, and they threw the tongues to the prisoners. When the prisoners got out of jail, they came to Canada. They'd had enough of Poland, and especially they'd had enough of being Jews in Poland. They took a boat to Canada and became tailors, every last one of them, except the ones that became dry cleaners. They lengthened pant cuffs and shortened pant cuffs, and they took in waists and let waists out. They could sew a new button on a shirt in under ten seconds. They made you a nice pair of pants.

My grandfather was born in a little village in Poland, a village where all the men had big white beards and wore black hats, and all the women had sad faces. Then he had a childhood and went to school for a few years, and then he learned how to sew, and then the war thing and the cows' tongues, and then he and his wife saved up a lot of money and clambered onto a boat to a place called Canada, which their cousin Isaac had written them about. They were barely into their twenties.

My grandfather saved a Polish bill so he could show it to his grandchildren, who turned out to be me and Jake. He could only save one of his bills, because he had to spend the rest so he and his wife could get out of Poland. The bill was called a zloty, maybe it was 50 of them, maybe 500. It had a picture of a young guy with black hair and a thin pointy nose. He didn't look at all like he was from one of those villages in Poland. Not at all like the old men in the photographs on the walls in our house.

My grandfather's teeth fell out of his mouth and he had to glue them back in every day. He also had to give himself a needle in his thigh every day because of his diabetes. He let me watch him as he sat there on the closed toilet seat with his pyjama bottoms down around his knees. He could talk to me about anything while he pushed a needle into the loose flesh of his thigh, just as if he wasn't doing anything at all.

Someday I would get old, and I would talk in a thick accent, and I would have to push a needle into my thigh.

If my grandfather had put his teeth out on the back porch, in a spumoni ice-cream container filled with water, the raccoons would have got them.

THUS DO HIS EYEBALLS RATTLE

When the bullet hit, the man stopped in mid-stride and mid-sentence and his stocky body stiffened. His eyes shot open in wonder, like he was trying to figure out what had happened. He was maybe thinking about the unfinished painting of Hitler in his basement. He was maybe thinking about dinner and how he'd never have one again. His hands tautened into claws, his stubby fingers curled. Then his knees buckled and his body caught up with them, slamming him forcefully onto the sidewalk in front of Faggot's Hardware. His right cheek struck the pavement and bounced a couple times, his dark, glassy eyes rattling in their sockets.

I could hear the rattling of his eyeballs. Like marbles clattering in those Seagram's whisky bags we kept marbles in when we were kids. Jake and I played marbles. We sat on the sidewalk and used our thumbs to flick our marbles at Rolf Köber's skull. If you got a marble into the hole in the side of his head, the hole made by the bullet that cut through the air from the gun my mother clutched, right through his hard hat, then you got to keep all the marbles that missed.

A woman screamed in the plaza parking lot, another woman with paper shopping bags spilling out of her arms, but my mother did not scream. I remember when they used to bring rides into this parking lot. There'd be a merry-go-round, a haunted house, bumper cars, a small Ferris wheel, and a very tame roller-coaster called the Caterpillar. Kids screamed on it when the canvas top came over the little cars and made everything dark. When a bullet goes into a man's head, everything also goes dark. And then the men walking with the man, they turn and run.

Rolf Köber's yellow hard hat spun like a dreidl in the air above the sidewalk, above all our heads. Mom dropped her gun, and it landed at her feet, clattering on the pavement. She was wearing the same black shoes she wore to synagogue on the rare occasions we went to synagogue. I used to like playing with my plastic soldiers on her shoe tree back at home, in the big closet in her bedroom. I'd hide the soldiers in her shoes, and under the arches of the high-heeled shoes, and I'd make screaming noises as the soldiers shot at each other. Their names were Mac and Charlie, always Mac and Charlie. They had plastic bases at their feet, so they could stand up. Real soldiers don't have plastic bases on their feet, which is why they fall down a lot. I learned this by watching CNN.

79

I watch CNN all the time now. I watch it obsessively — ever since the president with the dumb grin bombed Iraq and picked fleas out of the deposed dictator's hair. When I'm not watching CNN, like when I'm working or doing the dishes, I have it on in the background. I have since learned that real soldiers do not hide in shoes.

war = romanticized

I GET TO
TOUCH IT

Rachel and I were sitting in a campus pub with Chris and Carla, and they started talking about sex, which they always did, eventually. Even when they appeared in my dreams, they talked about nothing but sex.

In fact, this *was* a dream.

In this dream, Chris was going on about swingers' clubs up in Richmond Hill, an upscale suburb north of Toronto. He said he and Carla had attended a fetish evening at one of these clubs, which they had in real, waking life. And then Carla started talking about what it was like to have strange men touching her, and somehow Rachel stepped into the conversation, which was unusual for her, she never stepped into conversations, but this was a dream after all, and she said that I didn't know how to touch her breasts.

"What do you mean, I don't know how to touch your breasts?" I remember looking down into my hand and seeing a chicken wing perched there, and barbecue sauce all over my fingers, which I thought was strange, because I'm a vegetarian.

"You're always touching them, but you're no good at it. You touch my tits like you're polishing them. Like the way you polish the big samovar."

My father gave my mother a huge silver samovar for their twenty-fifth wedding anniversary. Then they were dead in the ground, first my mother and then my father, and I didn't want to sell it, though I knew I'd never actually use the thing. It meant nothing to Jake, of course, but I thought he should have it, too, we should both have it, so every year, on our parents' anniversary, we switch guardianship of it. Whenever I bring the samovar to Jake, he asks me what my name is, and then he asks me what the samovar is, and then he points to his closet and tells me put it in there, under some clothes, so no one will steal it. Whenever I have the samovar, I polish it like crazy. In fact, it's just

81

about the only thing I bother cleaning in my apartment. Everything else has cobwebs draped from it, except this enormous samovar.

But I didn't like the idea of Rachel telling Chris and Carla that I touched her breasts like I was polishing silver, and when we woke up, I told her so.

She started laughing. "I'd never tell Chris and Carla about how you touch me," she said, her body shaking with laughter as we lay side by side on my futon bed.

"Well, you did. Was that some kind of signal you were sending to me in my dreams to tell me what a lousy lover I am?"

Rachel laughed some more and reached for the glass of water she always kept by her side of my bed.

I reached for one of her breasts, and she pushed my hand away with her own free hand.

"No, really, let me touch it," I said. "Does it really feel like I'm trying to polish it? How come you've never told me before?"

She gulped down some water. "It was *your* dream! It wasn't real! I love the way you touch my breasts. You're like the world champion at touching my breasts."

I wasn't convinced. I reached again for her breast, and again she pushed my hand away. "See, you hate how I touch you. I can't believe you've never mentioned this before. You've just been gritting your teeth every time and hoping it'll end soon."

"No, it's just that I'm going to start laughing if you touch me right now. I'm all sensitive, just from talking about it." And she started laughing again.

"Great," I said, "now every time I touch you, you're going to think about my stupid dream and laugh. I should never have told you."

We were silent for a while. I lay on my back and Rachel lay on hers. Sometimes we lay on each other's back, but not this morning. I thought about the first time I touched her left breast, under her sweater and through her bra. The bra was thin and silky, and her nipple pushed thickly into it. I was so happy to find her nipple. I ran a fingertip around it and around it. The sun reached through the vertical blinds in thin stripes. In my living room, the phone rang. It stopped, and then it rang again. Outside, the garbage truck was creeping along the block, right by the three-storey house I rented the second floor of. We heard the clatter of emptied garbage cans being tossed back onto the sidewalk.

I reached for Rachel's chest, and on my palm I felt her nipple through her T-shirt. I really did love the way her breasts felt. I couldn't keep my hands off her. Even after we broke up, I kept thinking about her breasts, about the sensation of her nipple hard against my palm.

"Make them *really* shiny," she said.

THE VISIT

"Ben?"

"Ben."

"You're Ben, right?"

"Yup."

"I'm Jake."

"I know."

"Of course you're Ben. You always come here."

Jake was perched on the end of his unmade bed, and I sat across from him in the only chair in the room. It was a pretty nice room, even though there wasn't much in it. It was bright and had windows that opened up, and I'd put some of the paintings from Mom and Dad's house on the wall. On the little night table beside Jake's bed there was a black-and-white photograph of our mom and dad.

They're standing in a field, and Dad is wearing a long coat and Mom is wearing a hat, a dark jacket, and a skirt. There's also a photo of me and Jake together, a colour photo, back when he was a teenager and I wasn't one yet. We're sitting on the overstuffed sofa in the old living room and I'm smiling, while Jake looks really serious. I'm wearing a pair of white clam diggers and black running shoes with no socks. My T-shirt has the Jetsons on it. Jake is wearing a dark turtleneck and blue jeans. Maybe he was going on a date later.

"What's happening out there in the world, Ben?"

"I had an art opening downtown last night."

"Oh, you're an artist?"

"Yup."

"You paint — like those?" He pointed a thumb at the paintings on the wall behind him. Small things like that made me happy. Without looking, he knew there were paintings on the wall behind him.

"Something like that, Jake. Remember, like I told you last time, I'm a performance artist."

"Right! You eat doughnuts!" He laughed nervously, and we got up to go for a walk on the grounds. As with all the stray fragments he remembered, there was no logical explanation for why this one had stuck with him. His memory was sometimes good for as long as a couple of days, and then the slate would go blank again.

In the garden, everyone looked way worse than Jake. Some of them looked like shells, and some were disfigured. Born wrong. With some, I couldn't quite tell what was off, but I knew that something was. Like maybe the sides of their faces were reversed, with the left side on the right, and the right side on the left. Or the top on the bottom and the bottom on the top. My brother didn't seem to belong with these people, but the doctors had said there wasn't anywhere else to put him, unless I wanted to look after him full time.

"Hey, I saw Denise last week," I said.

Jake was kneeling down, looking at a snap-dragon with a ladybug on it. Every time he went for a walk outside, he saw things like snapdragons and ladybugs for the first time ever. That was the upside to his condition. "I know I should remember who Denise is, Ben, but I can't."

"You used to live with her, back when you were a journalist."

He laughed again. "I lived with her! I lived with a woman? Man, that's so good." He got up and shook his head. Then his mouth twisted and his face started to contort.

I put my arm around his shoulders and walked us on a little farther. His steps were heavy. Jake had been slim and athletic before his illness, but now he was bulky and awkward. "She loved you, Jake, and you loved her. Do you remember being in love?"

"I love it out here, Ben. How come we never come out here? Look at these incredible flowers! I've never seen anything like it!" Then he began crying, and I knew what he'd say next, because he always said it when we came out and saw flowers and he started crying. "I don't know why I'm crying."

I squeezed his shoulder. "Don't sweat it."

"Tell me about Denise, that lady who lived with me."

"She visited you last month, Jake. She still comes to see you."

Jake was silent. I could never decide if it was cruel for me to tell him about this thing he could never have again, or whether it might somehow make him feel good. He always wanted to know about her.

"She's very beautiful. She's a civil engineer. She's from Halifax, out east. You met her in Nicaragua about ten years ago and you fell in love. After her work down there was done, she moved to Toronto to be with you."

"Nicaragua." Jake looked down at his hands and shook his head, like he couldn't believe his hands had ever been in Nicaragua.

"This was before Dad died. Dad really liked her. You almost married her, but you wanted to get married in a synagogue and you couldn't find a rabbi who'd do it, because she wasn't Jewish."

"That's right, I'm Jewish, aren't I?"

"Yup, we're a couple of Jew-boys."

"Who are all these people?" He nodded his head towards the white, cast-iron benches we were passing.

"They live here, too. They're sick, but in a different way than you are. They've had really hard lives. Some of them have lived here since they were just little kids."

"And they remember?"

"I think most of them do. I think most of them remember."

"That's too bad for them. Some of them are so misshapen, their heads are all wrong, so maybe they remember how they got that way. That would be hard, to always remember that."

"You've got a friend here — do you remember his name?"

Jake drew his hand slowly through a spider web on a rose bush. "Man, this is so weird."

"His name is Carson. He looks after you around here."

"Johnny Carson." Jake laughed.

It drove me nuts that he remembered stupid things like that. If he had only so much room for memory, why did it have to be wasted on talk-show hosts?

"Topo Gigio!" He laughed some more.

And puppet mice.

Back in his room, I picked up the framed photo of Mom and Dad. "You remember them, right?"

He answered instantly. "That's Mom and Dad. They're dead."

"You know that they're my mother and father, too, right?"

"Sure. We both lived with them. We were a couple of Jew-boys."

"Do you remember the plaza near our house? Where we went to buy our *Archie* comics, and gum, and stuff?"

"Archie, Jughead, Veronica, Betty. Reggie Mantle. They built a snowman, didn't they? I remember them building a snowman."

"Do you remember what happened in that plaza?"

"Gum?"

"Yeah, what else?"

"Rides?"

"Sometimes they had rides there, like the Caterpillar. We went on the Caterpillar together. What else? When we got older, we visited Mom and she took us to the store with her. Do you remember?"

"We went on the Caterpillar, didn't we, Ben? Man, the top closed up and it was all dark in there."

"Yeah, but this was way later. Do you remember what happened?"

I wanted him to say it, but I didn't want to prompt him. I wanted him to tell me about the yellow hard hat that had hovered in thin air in front of Faggot's Hardware for a whole week.

The door to the room swung open a bit and a young blond guy in a blue uniform poked his head in. "Lunchtime, Jake!"

When the door closed again, my brother turned to me and said, "Who was that guy? I *know* that guy."

THE TWELVE RABBIS
OF, UM, OF, UH . . .

It was a morning so hot that my cheese sandwich was sweating and I couldn't eat it. I hadn't had any breakfast either, so I was dizzy. My eyelids were heavy and my face was flushed. Ira was at the desk just ahead of me, and when he turned around to look at me, I saw sweat streaming down his face.

At the front of the classroom, a stocky man in a black jacket and striped tie told us about the twelve rabbis who got threatened that if they didn't renounce their Judaism, they would meet horrible, unique deaths. This was a long time ago, though I never quite understood if it was the Biblical times in ancient Egypt or Assimilaria, or just the 1400s in Eastern Europe, maybe in Lodz, or Minsk, or Radom.

What I did understand was this: I had no idea what holiday we were supposed to be celebrating, but I knew the Christians got the twelve days of Christmas, where their true loves brought them partridges, turtle doves, and Johnny Sevens (with night-vision scope and bayonet!), and we got to sit around in a sweltering classroom in the basement of a synagogue listening to how twelve rabbis got killed because they refused to give up their Torah, their Talmud, their tefillin.

I was dizzy-headed as I listened to the stocky man. A fly buzzed past my ear and landed on my sweating cheese sandwich. The bread was white, and the cheese was orange, and the fly was dark grey. A piece of lined white paper lay on the small wooden desk in front of me, and a pencil, too. Every one of us children in the classroom had been given a sheet of paper and a pencil, and we had printed our names at the top in Hebrew letters, right to left.

I didn't even think synagogues were open on Sundays, but here we were. This was something called Special Programming, which sounded frightening. I had never attended Special Programming before, and I was never to attend it again. Why now, on the hottest day of the year, while my parents took my grandmother for a drive to the country? At the top of one wall of the classroom, near the ceiling, was a row of small rectangular windows. They were cranked open, and sun poured in. Above us, banks of fluorescent lights glowed harshly, flickering every now and then. I felt like lying my head down on my desk and going to sleep.

They said to the first rabbi, If you give up Judaism, we will let you live; if you do not, you will die a terrible, painful death. The rabbi didn't hesitate: he would never abandon his God. They threw him from the top of a cliff and he didn't even scream as he plummeted to the craggy rocks below.

They said to the second rabbi, Say that you will no longer be a Jew, and we will spare your life. The rabbi refused to renounce his people, and he prepared himself for the long fall to death. Instead, they tied him up and lowered him into a vat of boiling oil. He died in silence.

They said to the third rabbi, Look, man, you've seen what happened to your two friends; worship a bronze calf or something and you will live to see your children grow up. The rabbi clutched his prayer book and shook his head, almost imperceptibly. He was then shredded to ribbons with a giant metal comb.

By then, I'd gotten the idea: none of these rabbis were going to convert. They were stubborn and they were brave. Judaism was more important than anything, and life would be worthless anyway without their God, their traditions, their late nights of debating Talmud by candlelight. I got the idea. Now could we be let out of this furnace room in the basement of the synagogue?

They said to the fourth rabbi, Renounce your god and we will grant you life; otherwise, you die a terrifically painful death. The rabbi, again, didn't even need to think about it. He said he would never betray the God of the Chosen People. He was chosen to die by fire, bound to a stake. You could tell that he was praying silently, one last time, as the flames turned his body to a charcoal pillar.

They said to the fifth rabbi, Give up this thing of being a Jew and you shall live; otherwise, your death will be instant and messy. The rabbi crossed his arms over his chest, his tallit swaying gently in defiance. A ten-ton concrete block crashed down on him.

They said to the sixth rabbi, You have seen the fate met by those who refuse to convert; what is your choice, you fool? The rabbi said, *Baruch atah adonai eloheynu*, but before he got to *melech ha'olum*, a stake was drilled through his heart.

We were halfway through the story of the Twelve Rabbis when I started feeling really guilty. I imagined walking home from school one day, and getting cornered by some Christian boys. I pictured them wearing Boy Scout outfits. They say to me, Ben, give up your Jewish god and become Christians like us, or we'll kill you right now. I think of potato latkes and jelly fruit slices, and of my grandfather's dentures floating in a glass by the sink, and of my mother sitting on the edge of my bed and telling me how all her aunts and uncles were killed by Hitler, and of my father slathering horseradish upon his lump of gefilte fish at the Passover Seder, and of my mother getting pelted with snowballs because she's four years old and she speaks Yiddish. Then I think of being dead.

Nothing happens when you're dead, and you're not even aware that nothing is happening, because you're dead.

The reason I feel guilty is because I don't think I would be as brave as those rabbis.

They said to the seventh rabbi, You must give up your dirty religion, old man, or thou shalt be smote in an unthinkably unpleasant manner. The rabbi stroked his beard, not because he was giving the choice any thought, but because he was proud of his beard and this would be his last chance to touch it. They fed him to an alligator and he died in silence.

They said to the eighth rabbi, If you refuse to turn your back on your temple, we will be forced to kill you. The rabbi refused to turn his back thusly, and they stuffed his mouth full of asps and sewed shut his lips.

They said to the ninth rabbi, You will deny your ludicrous god, or you will suffer a death even a dog is too good for. The rabbi hung his head and prayed to his God, rocking on his feet, his eyes closed. They buried him to his neck and invited townspeople to pummel his head with stones.

If I didn't get some air soon, I would faint. The man in the black jacket finally loosened his striped tie and paused. His lips were quivering. He wiped his brow. I was willing to become a goy in exchange for a steady cool breeze and a large glass of ice water. The clock was beginning to melt.

They said to the tenth rabbi, Rip your prayer book to pieces and never set foot again in your temple, and you live to be an old man. The rabbi said that that would be impossible. They inflicted a hundred tiny cuts upon his flesh, with a leisurely pause between each wound. He died before they'd finished.

They said to the eleventh rabbi, Don't be a fool — no god can be worth the pain you shall experience if you do not convert. The rabbi said that he had lived by the Torah and he would die for it. They set starving wolves upon him to eat of his flesh.

We gasped for air as we awaited the fate of the twelfth rabbi. Would there be a punchline to this story?

Perhaps this rabbi, having witnessed the unspeakable deaths of eleven of his fellows, would accept the demands of his persecutors, while continuing inwardly to be a Jew.

Perhaps this rabbi would turn and make a break for it, using deft judo chops to the throat to vanquish those who tried to block his path.

Perhaps this rabbi would cast his face towards the heavens, and a great storm would lash out from God and kill all his persecutors.

They said to the twelfth rabbi, You have seen the unenviable fates of the other eleven Jews who chose to cling to your powerless god; we know that you are the most brilliant rabbi in the land; finally we have come to a rabbi who can use logic to overcome his internal evil; look around you — there is no other Jew to witness your decision: do you choose your impotent god over life?

It had been only a few years earlier that I had read a book about five blind Chinese brothers who touch different parts of an elephant, and when asked to describe what the elephant is like, the one touching the elephant's trunk says it's long and snake-like; the one touching the elephant's side says it's like an enormous boulder; the one touching the elephant's ear says it's like a lilypad; the one touching the elephant's tail says it's like a reed in a swamp; the one touching the elephant's eyeball says it's like a jellyfish. I liked that story a lot more.

The rabbi replied, I like how I'm a Jew.

They strapped him to a rocket and launched it into the sun.

While Sidney and I waited outside the synagogue for our parents to come pick us up, the sky clouded over and rain began to fall. The sweat in our clothes turned to rainwater. It was a miracle.

ANTS
WITH PLANS

adult on the ground
linking death of bugs to Holocaust-
distancing?

On my hands and knees, on the sidewalk, in the sun, I watched the undulating mass of red ants crawling all over each other, chaotic, mechanical, glistening.[Each of those ants knew exactly where it was going. Or if not, it would find out when it got there.]The sun was like a huge magnifying glass funnelling light directly onto us, me and the ants.

Kids on two legs passed by me while I crouched on all fours watching ants on their sixes, and I knew that times had changed. When I was a child and I'd found one of these incredible civilizations in between the square pink patio bricks in our backyard, I'd run to the fridge and pull out a bowl of green Jell-O, there was always Jell-O at hand back then, and I'd plop a big glob on the ant

colony. I could look right through the green J
and see the ants, frozen in flight like the cit
of Pompeii.

I liked looking at the pictures of the fleeing citizens of Pompeii in my *National Geographic* magazine. *Munus! Ingens munus!* Their arms were
flexed and their legs bent, just like they were jog-
ging to Yorkdale mall, where I used to like to go
check out the lizards in the pet shop. The citizens
of Pompeii had no warning when the huge glob
of green Jell-O came hurtling out of Vesuvius and
plopped down on them. They were frozen in their
poses of escape for centuries.

I imagined that in tiny ant magazines, centuries
from now, the ants I had killed would be depicted in
artful photo spreads. Worker ants, frozen in time,
caught in mid-scurry, perfectly preserved for ant
archaeologists, and ant anthropologists, and ant
journalists labouring feverishly in a world devoid of
human life. I mean, this would be after the nuclear
holocaust, which would wipe out all humans, but
leave intact the insects, my grandfather's teeth, and
my Hardy Boys books, including *The Case of the
Missing Patriarchal Capitalist Society*.

The Jell-O siege was the humane alternative to the much slower and far less pleasant slaughter of ants, one by one, with a magnifying glass. I didn't want to actually cook the ants and watch them writhe in pain as their limbs incinerated. I didn't get any pleasure from that. My mom also said that Jell-O was refreshing, as she plunked down each of our bowls after a roast-beef dinner, and I had felt that I was giving the ants a refreshing death, a lime-flavoured death.

Now, though, crouching on the sidewalk across the road from the strip mall where my mother had assassinated Rolf Köber while cancer ate her body, I only observed the ants. I had absolutely no impulse to kill them. I wondered how many there were, and I pictured the strata beneath the earth's surface that was teeming with ants: red ones and black ones, and even brown ants. It amazed me that none of the children returning from school stopped to kneel beside me on the sidewalk and watch the ants. Kids didn't watch ants anymore. They had other things to watch.

The frenetic cluster of red ants was like a shifting mass of molasses. I knew that if I extended one finger and placed the tip just over the little ant mountain, they would stream up my hand, and my arm, and my neck, ribbons of red ants flowing in reverse rivulets up my body, like raindrops streaking upward on the passenger window of a car. Like a humming blanket of ants covering Charlton Heston as, teeth clenched tight, he fought like hell to save his plantation, goddammit.

I couldn't imagine my mother actually pulling the trigger of a gun, or even knowing how. I couldn't imagine her putting down her Dominion bags and drawing a gun from the big pocket of her camel-coloured coat, and pointing the gun, and shooting a man in the head.

But when I *remembered* her doing it, then I could imagine.

105

remember what you can't believe

- second generation Holocaust lit

- his world in Canada, but is he relieved or guilty about it?

JOURNEYS
OUT OF THE
BODY

I was bobbing against the ceiling, peering down at myself lying in bed on my back, sleeping, sweating, and all my friends were at school. I lay buried in my bedsheets, eyes closed, mouth open. Even though I had absolutely no interest in hockey, my bedsheets had little pictures of hockey players on them — Toronto Maple Leafs, the old blue sweater, maybe Dave Keon and Norm Ullman, Ron Ellis, Mike Walton, Eddie Shack, Johnny Bower in the net. George Armstrong holding up the Stanley Cup. I had no interest in hockey, but I couldn't avoid it, because it was on right after *My Favorite Martian*, and everyone else in my family loved it. My dresser was covered in plastic model airplanes, colourful rubbery creatures from my Strange

Change Machine, and a few half-eaten Incredible Edibles. My bedroom window was covered with a thin layer of frost, through which the mid-morning sunlight streamed in crazy angles, bouncing off the walls like ricocheting bullets.

I found that if I fluttered my feet gently, as if I were swimming, I could propel myself slowly across the room, my shoulder blades brushing the ceiling. Down below, on the bed, my nostrils were red and raw, and I clutched a crumpled Kleenex in my right fist. Balled-up Kleenexes littered my bed, my night table, the floor. A cup of clear tea my mother had brought me earlier in the morning, before she went to open her shop, sat shivering on the night table, beside a face-down hardcover copy of *The Black Stallion Returns*. Walter Farley was my favourite writer, better even than Franklin W. Dixon, whose blue-spined Hardy Boys novels took up almost a full shelf in my bookcase. Jake had told me that there *was* no Franklin W. Dixon, that he was a committee of writers, but I didn't believe him. How could Franklin W. Dixon not exist? — I could *picture* him.

I swam over to the bookcase and found that, by pushing my feet gently against the ceiling, I could glide down to the level of my Hardy Boys books. I reached out with one hand and ran my fingertips across the spines: *The Secret Agent on Flight 101, While the Clock Ticked, The Mystery of the Aztec Warrior, Murder in the Old Bell Tower, The Secret of the Lost Tunnel, The Short-Wave Mystery,* which was the first one I'd read, *The Ghost at Skeleton Rock, Footprints Under the Window, The Nazi at the Hardware Store, The Masked Monkey, The Missing Chums, The Bombay Boomerang, Danger on Vampire Trail, The Case of the Disappearing Catfish, The Clue of the Hissing Serpent.* I'd read them all, and I'd read them to my grandmother while she fried up some chicken fat and onions for me after we watched champagne bubbles float through the air on *Lawrence Welk.*

I swam past my stuffed closet to the window, my forehead bouncing against the glass. I had never actually swum out the window, over the lawns and the houses, and didn't know how far I could get before I snapped back into my sleeping body. I wondered if I'd get lost out there. Things looked so different from up above than they did from on the ground.

I'd read about people who astral projected and swam into other worlds while their bodies lay in sleep. They visited with other levitating travellers and maybe even met some girls floating around and had astral sex with them, way up in the air, or in that other world. I hadn't even had sex on earth yet, so the idea appealed to me.

But when I reached an astral hand towards the lock on top of the window, before I even discovered if an astral hand could manipulate a corporeal lock, I woke up with a boner. I trapped it between my thighs, and yelled for my mom to bring me a glass of cold ginger ale. But the house was empty. Even Frank and Joe Hardy couldn't help me now.

THE HOUSE
ON PANNAHILL,
STILL STANDING THERE

After the shiva for my father came to an end —
all those bagels consumed, the egg salad, the cold
cuts, all that coffee, the exhaustion of mourning,
the relatives whose names I didn't remember, the
slow sad shaking of heads, the watery eyes staring
into my own, the serene confusion on Jake's face,
the men wrapped in tefillin so early in the morning,
the rabbi's reassuring hand on my shoulder, the
afternoons that felt like 3 a.m. — I gathered my
car keys and walked out the door. It was always
like entering another world to leave the house after
a shiva. Like coming back to a distant country
whose language I'd almost forgotten. I looked at
the people on the sidewalks, moving along as if on

conveyor belts. Their lives, somehow, had gone on in my absence.

At first I was driving aimlessly, and then I realized I was heading north, heading towards Bathurst Manor. I passed Eglinton, Glencairn, Lawrence, Wilson, Sheppard. I cut across Wilmington and soon I was in the old neighbourhood. I slowed right down across from the house on Pannahill Road, my foot tight on the brake. The amazing thing was, each time I visited, the street got smaller and smaller. The house, on the other hand, got steadily bigger.

Where there had been just a tiny porch at the door, good only for leaving a newspaper or a jug of milk, or fumbling for my keys in the dark or wiping my boots on the mat, there was now a vast verandah stretching across the front of the house, with an ornate cast-iron table surrounded by matching chairs.

And the driveway, which had been wide enough for only one car, usually a station wagon, the old blue Valiant, was now wide enough for two cars, though the garage itself could still fit only one. My friends and I had conducted circuses in that garage, and sold fossils of trilobites, and did read-ings of the poems of Tennyson and Ogden Nash, half a league onward and liquor is quicker, and put on little plays based on TV shows like *My Favorite Martian* and *The Time Tunnel*. The garage smelled of oil, and damp newspapers, and dust. Centipedes raced across its concrete floor.

I wondered if the red-brick barbecue my father had built was still standing in the backyard. And whether the patio was still there: where I'd dumped blobs of green Jell-O onto black ants emerging from between the pink clay tiles. I put the car into park, in front of where the Cohens had once lived — Sheldon and Eileen Cohen and their three daughters who taunted me and, in a way I didn't understand, excited me — and I stepped out onto the street. I wondered if the street remembered my feet, but I was sure the surface was new. Perhaps there'd been several new surfaces since the days I'd played road hockey there with Sammy and Ira. Our two blocks really had shrunk: I was nearly bigger than Pannahill now, but in turn I was dwarfed by the house.

I walked slowly up the driveway. The house was quiet, its heavy curtains pulled neatly shut. Behind that small window beside the garage was the green porcelain sink where my grandfather had placed the glass that held his bobbing teeth. Above the garage was Jake's room. When he wasn't home I would crouch beneath the window and peer out between the curtains at the Cohen girls. They had the sprinkler going on their front lawn and they ran around in circles, leaping through the fine spray in their T-shirts and shorts. They laughed while they ran, and they shrieked. First, Mindy Cohen chased Debi Cohen, then they suddenly switched and Debi Cohen chased Mindy Cohen. Then Susie Cohen burst onto the porch in a red one-piece swimsuit, and they shrieked some more. Next door, the Coluccis' black terrier strained against his chain, barking at them.

I began to walk around the side of my old house, along a narrow stone path, likely the same one my bare feet had padded along three decades earlier. As I came to the back of the house, I could see immediately everything had changed. Where once there was just the patio, a barbecue, a weeping

113

willow, and a wooden porch leading out to the laundry line from the kitchen, there were now trellises, cobblestone paths, and luxurious gardens that looked almost tropical. It was an entire village now. Everything seemed to be throbbing. In the distance, I heard the buzzing of power lines, the chirping of crickets, the drone of a plane overhead.

I paused and waited to see if I'd been spotted — if the new people of 179 Pannahill would come out and demand to know what I was doing there. I wondered how many families had lived here since we had, how many kids had slept in my bedroom, how many grandparents had died in the room downstairs, their dentures bobbing in glasses of cloudy water, the sounds of the Lawrence Welk Orchestra leaking quietly from the old RCA Victor television set.

But nobody came out of the house. Nobody came out of any of the houses on the street. I realized that I hadn't seen any cars in the driveways, and I hadn't seen a single person since I'd turned onto the street. I listened again. Now, there was only silence. It was a ghost town. It was like a movie where there'd been an atomic war and everything looked so normal, you knew it wasn't normal.

I walked a little further into the backyard. I'd played croquet in this backyard, clacked the green wooden ball against the red wooden ball. I'd played *Man from U.N.C.L.E.* with Ira. In this backyard, I'd watched my father build his barbecue. I knew he could do all sorts of mysterious things with his T-square, his vise, and his hacksaw in the basement, but I didn't know he could actually construct a small building of brick.

Peering through bushes and gardens, I saw finally that the barbecue wasn't gone — not completely. Where it once stood, there were now several uneven layers of its red-brick foundation, as if the cluster of flowering bushes bursting from it had shattered the structure. It was like Greek ruins. I approached it, knelt down, and ran my fingertips along the bricks. My father had touched those very bricks, had settled them into place, had made us steaks and hamburgers that tasted of Worcestershire sauce and charcoal.

I whispered to my father as if I were kneeling by his grave. I reported to him that his barbecue was still here, or evidence of his barbecue, at least. But that everything else was different in our backyard. The willow was gone, the wooden porch had been torn down, and the checkerboard patio had been replaced by a garden of stones, flowering bushes, and cast-iron archways.

My dad said it was no big deal, it was their house now, those who lived there, and they could do what they wanted with it. He wondered, though, whether our Valiant was still in the driveway.

I told him the driveway was empty, but the Valiant was long gone anyway, wasn't it?

He laughed and said he was only kidding, but it was that laugh of his that meant he wasn't really kidding, he'd just been confused.

When you're dead, you get confused easily.

DRAGON'S PARADISE

My grandmother fried up some chicken skin and chicken fat with onions and we sat in front of the TV and watched *Lawrence Welk*. Then we played cards — Fish and War. Then we sat on her balcony and gazed out across the suburbs from the ninth floor, and sometimes I'd look down into the streets and pick out Volkswagens. It was a game Jake and I played when we were on road trips with our parents — you got one point for every Volkswagen you spotted, and if it was red, you got two. Red Bug! Fried chicken skin and chicken fat with onions was my favourite food. Sometimes we called it *grevin* and sometimes we called it *schmaltz*, which just meant "fat."

My grandmother spoke pretty good English, in her heavy Russian accent. She said she hadn't spoken a word of Russian since she'd left that country in 1917. She hadn't spoken Russian in half a century.

When he was alive, my grandfather spoke Yiddish with her, and sometimes they spoke Yiddish to my dad. He could understand it, but he couldn't speak it back to them, except maybe a few words. When my grandfather was alive, the three of us often sat and watched *Lawrence Welk*. Lawrence Welk spoke with an accent, too, but I didn't know what kind. I was in kindergarten back then, and I didn't like watching the *Lawrence Welk Show*, except for the part with the bubbles. I wanted shows with puppets. I liked Ed Sullivan's puppet mouse, Topo Gigio, and I liked the little puppet mouse on *Chez Hélène*, even though it spoke French and I didn't understand anything it said, except maybe a few words, like *bonjour* and *mon ami*, which meant "my little mouse."

While my grandmother and I sat out on the balcony, nine floors up, we talked about all sorts of things, but there were some things she didn't want to talk about.

For example:

When I mentioned Russia, my grandmother spat.

When I mentioned Germans, my grandmother spat.

When I mentioned Dean Martin, my grandmother spat. She didn't like that he was making movies with almost-naked women in them.

About the Germans, she spat because they had killed all her brothers and sisters.

About Russia, she spat for reasons that I didn't yet understand.

After we'd watched *Lawrence Welk* and played cards and sat on the balcony, and after I'd snacked on some crispy, juicy *schmaltz*, we went down the elevator of her apartment building and across the road, to Dragon's Paradise, to eat some Chinese food. Dragon's Paradise was situated between a cigar store, where I went afterwards to buy some potato chips and an *Archie* comic, and a shoe repair store. Mr. Tam, who owned Dragon's Paradise and brought the food to our table, knew a few words of Yiddish. He and my grandmother would banter a bit, then look at me and laugh. I'd laugh, too.

It was funny seeing Yiddish words come out of a Chinese face.

Here are the things we ate at Dragon's Paradise:

- sweet and sour spareribs, which I often got sauce from on my shirt and then my grandmother would wipe at me with a serviette
- chicken fried rice, which I liked, except for the little green onions
- chicken chow mein, which I liked, except for when I got a crunchy piece of chicken — "I got some beak," I'd tell my grandmother
- egg foo yung with mushrooms and onions, which I liked the taste of, but was suspicious of because it might be healthy due to the eggs
- egg rolls, which I liked and also it had nothing to do with eggs.

Then we ate our fortune cookies. I had to read my grandmother her fortune because she couldn't read English. Sometimes a cookie would have two fortunes in it, and sometimes these would be the same fortune, while other times they would be different. My grandmother explained to me that if the two fortunes were the same, it was because the machinery in the fortune-cookie factory wasn't working too good and the fortunes got stuck together. But if the fortunes were different, it was because the workers were lazy and thought they could get through their work faster if they stuffed extra fortunes into each cookie. For my grandmother, you could only be broken or lazy.

On the wall of Dragon's Paradise were giant framed photos of China. No one in the photos was ever eating Chinese food. While we sat in the restaurant eating, other old people would come over to our table and speak to my grandmother in Yiddish. They'd mess up my hair and squeeze my cheek and say in English to me that I was becoming a big boy and I had nice curly hair, if only they had such curls themselves, any girl would want to have curls like mine, what nice curls. Then they'd talk Yiddish again to my grandmother, and suddenly the mood would change. They'd speak in loud whispers, and my grandmother would shake her head sadly.

I know now that it was people dying they were talking about. When people got old like my grandmother, they had something wrong with part of their guts, and they died, and got stuck into the ground.

INTERVIEW
WITH A
HARD HAT

On a cold, dreamless night, I drifted out from beneath my bedsheets and through my closed window. I manoeuvred between some telephone lines and rose above the treetops. There weren't many lights on in the bungalows and triplexes below, and not a single vehicle was moving along the narrow streets.

Snow sailed past me and through me, reflecting the dim light of the moon in a sky smudged with clouds. I didn't feel cold, though; I still felt as warm as if I were burrowed beneath my blankets. On a whim, I turned north, leaving the outer edges of downtown and soaring gently above midtown. Still, not a car on the roads. Below me I saw the Beth Tzedec, one of the most beautiful Orthodox synagogues in the city, and a few blocks farther north the Holy Blossom, an equally beautiful Reform synagogue whose name always made me think of a Chinese restaurant. I couldn't remember whether I'd ever been to either. I wondered whether I'd been to more synagogues or more Chinese restaurants in this city. I could see through the roofs of the temples into the sanctuaries. Only a dim light emanated from the altars in each, and a glow from the ark, where the Torahs were kept. Reflexively, I patted my head, checking for a yarmulke, but I wasn't actually *inside* the synagogues, so it didn't count.

124

Still farther north, I saw a vehicle bisecting the city from the east. It moved slowly, with deliberation, its headlights boring cylinders of light into the dark street ahead. As it neared, I could make out a red light on its roof. The light flashed gently and rhythmically, and then I knew what I was looking at. My father lay on his back in the ambulance, and I knelt beside him. I strained to hear what I was saying, or what he was saying, but it was no use. I watched myself stroke my father's thin arm and I watched my lips move.

The ambulance cut across Bathurst and I continued my path towards the city's north end. For a moment, I felt as if someone had grabbed me, or hugged me, but it was only some wisps of cloud. I hadn't realized I'd risen so high. The snow was heavier here, but I still felt warm. The synagogue where I'd had my bar mitzvah came into view, partially obscured by some trees. The other kid's voice cracked when he sang, but my voice had already changed. After we'd recited our portions of the Old Testament, our *parshas*, and did that thing of parading around the temple carrying the Torah, while people craned from their seats to touch their prayer books or tallitim to its scrolls and then kiss them, there were a whole bunch more prayers, and some songs, and Bernie — that was the other kid's name — and I sat up there behind the rabbi till the endless service had ended.

After that, old men shuffled around in an adjoining room, cupping white serviettes filled with chickpeas in their palms. And in the banquet room, the bar mitzvah guests filed in for some wine, some lunch. Jake made a funny speech about me and everybody laughed and clapped. My friends and I posed for photos. Relatives I'd never seen before kissed me.

Men pressed cheques into my hand and I stuffed them into the pocket of my blazer. And then I went home to sleep. I felt like I'd been awake for three days straight.

It was years later and it was nighttime. I rose from my bedsheets and drifted out my closed window. I had arrived at Bathurst Manor Plaza, and was gliding slowly over its empty parking lot. Here, my feet became heavy and I found myself sinking. A thin layer of snow covered the pavement below me, so I couldn't even see the white and yellow lines that told you where to park and where not to park.

As I came nearly level with the roofs of the stores, I saw a yellow ball spinning above Faggot's Hardware. Drifting closer, I saw that it wasn't a ball at all — it was a hard hat. Had it really been floating up here for a decade?

I reached out, tentatively, and placed my hands on its surface. The hard hat came to a stop.

"Hey, I can hold you," I said to it.

"Hey," the hard hat replied.

I turned it in my hands. There was the jagged black insignia. There was the black-singed bullet hole, where the bullet from the gun my mother had held got past Rolf Köber's feeble protection and entered his skull.

"I gotta say, this is pretty weird that you can talk. You're a yellow helmet. You don't even have a mouth."

"Yeah, but it's pretty weird that you're floating around in the middle of the night, isn't it?"

"So you've just been hovering here for the last ten years?"

"Sometimes kids go into the cigar store down there and buy some licorice or maybe a *Sad Sack* comic, and then they come out and throw rocks at me, try to knock me out of the air."

The strangest thing was that I remembered that hard hat falling. I remembered it landing right beside Rolf Köber's head and bouncing on the sidewalk in front of the hardware store.

"You remember who did this?" I asked the hard hat. "Who pulled the trigger?"

I drew my hands gently away from the hard hat and it began to slowly spin again, right there in the air.

"It's a bit of a blur to me," the hard hat said. "It's like a dream. I mean, I don't think I even started thinking about stuff till I got up here. Before that I was just a helmet on some asshole's head."

This was convenient. I didn't know whether the hard hat was lying or on the level. I had no idea when hard hats had achieved consciousness, or whether they were even capable of it when they were on someone's head.

"So you don't even remember? You don't remember the bullet going through you and killing the Nazi? You don't remember my mom standing there holding the gun with both hands, looking like she could barely believe what she'd just done?"

The hard hat spun silently in the cool night air. The moon glinted off it, or maybe it was the streetlights.

"Thing is," I explained, "Mom was dying of cancer. She figured it wouldn't make any difference if she took Rolf Köber with her. Some kids threw snowballs at her when she was a little kid, just because she was Jewish. I mean, she was only about four years old and she could just speak

Yiddish. Also, she never got to meet most of her relatives, because they died in the camps."

Later, after I'd snapped back into my body, after the me in the clouds lined up with the me in the bed, I worried that the hard hat might have thought I meant summer camps instead of concentration camps.

THE ESSAY BESIDE DAD'S BOWLING BALL

In Dad's walk-in closet, there were lots of clothes, including all those shirts that I salvaged and still wear. It takes a lot for me to throw away a shirt that was once my father's, that my father walked around in, but when more than one button has fallen off, and the cuffs are frayed, and a hole has formed at the breast pocket, and there are ink stains on the sleeve, I have one fewer shirt that my father wore against his skin.

But in his closet, there were other things, too: bank statements and cancelled cheques that stretched back two decades or more; a collection of little soap bars from motels; hundreds of books of matches; and purple velvet bags that contained tefillin. There were several of these: my father's own, his father's, my mother's father's, a more modern one that must have belonged to Jake, and one where the tefillin straps were so short, it must have belonged to a child. This reminded me of when you see a funeral for a kid, or photographs from one, and the coffin is so tiny, it breaks your heart. Or on TV, where there's been a tragedy in some poor country, and they show a row of blanket-covered bodies, and the people milling around are holding their noses and swatting away flies, and one of the blankets is so small it might just be a tea towel, though I don't think they have luxuries like tea towels in such countries.

131

But this tefillin kit was like that. And I imagined that it had belonged to an uncle of my father's, or even an uncle of one of my grandparents, and that uncle had been taken to a concentration camp and somehow his tefillin was salvaged. I thought of those instructional line drawings I'd been shown as a child, where some clean-cut boy goes through the stages of putting on his tefillin. He wears a white shirt and his left sleeve is rolled up. When he gets to the part where he puts the little box on his forehead, and the leather straps hang past each of his cheeks, he looks like an old man.

Also in my father's closet I found a bulging cardboard box that contained electronic equipment that had become obsolete: a couple of telephone answering machines; an adding machine practically the size of a small car; some transistor radios; a reel-to-reel tape recorder, with a pile of tapes I still intend to listen to, because I'm certain they contain the voices of Mom and Dad, and maybe other people, too, unless the magnetic stuff has worn out; some dome-like structure with a brush attached, which maybe had something to do with cleaning shoes; a small blue electric blanket that I lay over my mom when she wasn't feeling too well because of her cancer; some big headphones; a travel clock that folded out of a brown leatherette case and had glowing green numbers. Like the tefillin, I kept all this stuff, and thought I might use it in a performance someday.

Up on the shelf above my father's hanging clothes, I found two bowling balls in leather bags with handles. Beside those was a transparent plastic bag containing papers of various sizes and colours.

I took this down, sat on the floor of the walk-in closet, and stuffed my hand in. I found documents from my childhood, things my mother had obviously saved — mainly birthday cards I had made for her. There were also a couple of projects in there that I wrote in elementary school, like one on pygmies and another about Louis Riel, plus a speech about how Toronto's new city hall looked like something out of science fiction, which it did when I was in elementary school, plus a speech about our black poodle Rufus and how smart he was, just like a human, book reports about books like *The Black Stallion* and *Henry Huggins*, and also an essay I'd forgotten about called "The Snowball." It was hand-printed in pencil on blue-lined paper and held together by a paper clip in its top left corner. The paper around the paper clip was rusted brown.

Sitting on the floor of my father's walk-in closet, I started reading.

"When people don't like Jews it is called anti-Semitism. Anti-Semitism is the hatred of Jews and it goes back in history. The Jews got chased from everywhere they lived, for example back when they lived in Egypt. Mostly they couldn't bring their belongings with them. Also, they were running so much, they didn't have time to rest so they had to eat matzoh, which was faster to make. At times that they ran out of food and didn't even have time to make matzoh a miracle happened and matzoh fell from heaven to feed them.

"Jewish people can't trust anyone else but other Jewish people. Christians will stab you in the back if there is some emergency. It is okay to have Christian friends but be careful they don't stab you in the back. This is why Jews have to stick together and also should marry only other Jews.

"When my mother was a little girl, she got thrown a snowball at by a Christian boy. Although it hurt her to have snowballs hit her in the head, it made her proud to be Jewish because you really have to struggle to be Jewish so you really believe in it.

"Many famous people are Jewish: Danny Kaye.

"Later, Hitler started a war because he wanted to kill all the Jewish people in the world, starting with in Europe. His Nazi soldiers rounded up Jews and put them in big concentration camps and then divided up the weak from the healthy and put the weak in ovens or used poison gas on them when they thought they were taking a shower.

"Hitler killed six million Jews. Many got away and came to Canada and the United States, but six million was most of them. If it wasn't for the Second World War, I would have a much bigger family. It is good that my grandparents came to Canada or else they would have been killed with their brothers and sisters. I wouldn't have been born ever and Jake either.

"The Jewish people have invented many things and have been important in history. Israel is a place where Jewish people can be safe."

I had no memory of writing any of this, but I couldn't say that I disagreed with it. This little essay might be something I could use for a performance-art project, like the bowling balls and the old electronics. On the bottom right-hand corner of the last page, in red pen, was an A and the words "Well-written, Ben! Ben is an asset to the class."

ARCTIC
EXPEDITION

The phone rang just after one in the morning. I was lying in the king-size bed in my hotel room in downtown Yellowknife, just off Franklin Avenue, propped up on a heap of pillows, reading a huge hardcover book about Gilbert and George that I'd dragged along. I had to come up with something for the Cleveland Performance Art Festival by the end of the week, when the proposals were due, and I was looking for inspiration, for a trigger. Reading about other artists' projects often gave me ideas for my own.

I was also drunk, after a long night at the Raven's Pub, and then the Gold Range, where almost everyone else was Aboriginal. The guy at the hotel desk called the Gold Range the Strange

Range. Everyone there danced, except me. Bare tree branches scraped against my window and the guests in the room above made love noisily. I could hear them over their blaring television.

I had barely finished saying "Hello" into the receiver when my father starting talking, his voice slow and tired.

"Ben, we were out on the boat, we were just out on the boat, I'm so sorry, I promised your mother I'd look after you guys, that everything would be okay, but we were out on the boat and Jake was just saying how it was getting a bit dark and we should probably head back in and then he just stopped talking and was looking at me like he didn't know me, or more like he didn't know he was looking at me, didn't know I was there. He was really pale, Ben, his face and his lips were all white, but he'd just been pulling a fish off the hook, a rock bass, only a minute earlier, and he was saying we should bring the boat in.

"Then he was all sweaty and lying on the floor of the boat and I had trouble getting the motor started, but then I got it started and the rental guy helped me get him out of the boat and into my car and I drove him to the hospital. I drove as fast as I could, Ben, but maybe I should have called an ambulance, I don't know, so they could work on him, hook him up to things, while they took him to Emergency."

Jake was four years older than me and worked as a journalist for a wire service and a few magazines in Canada and England. I was thinking that he was dead, that what my father was telling me was that my brother Jake was dead, but I didn't want to ask. I was thinking about how we'd be looking at coffins in the morning. We'd be talking to rabbis and lawyers and the guy in the bank where Jake had his accounts. Phoning up Regina's Foods to see if we could get a few trays of bagels and cream cheese, some egg salad and some chopped liver, for the gathering at Dad's place after the funeral. It didn't seem long since we'd gone through that for Mom.

I was staring at a photo of Gilbert and George wearing matching gold-lamé smoking jackets and standing by a huge red wing chair. We used to have a huge green wing chair at the house on Pannahill, and Jake and I climbed it like it was a mountain. It *was* a mountain. When Jake made an avalanche noise, we'd rock the wing chair all over the place and hang on for dear life. Sometimes it was also a ship in a storm or a plane going through turbulence and we were clinging on to the wings. We made thunder noises with our mouths.

"Ben, he's hanging in there, but it's not looking good. The doctors can't tell if he's in a coma or unconscious, but he's burning up, his whole body is burning up like he's on fire, he's got some kind of crazy fever."

Jake was alive. My father was sobbing. I was in Yellowknife.

"Ben, hold on, the doctor wants to speak to me again. Just hold on, don't go anywhere."

I was in Yellowknife, in the Northwest Territories, the Arctic, where they'd flown me in as a performance-artist-in-residence for a couple of weeks. I was visiting schools and colleges, and going to community centres, and I'd be doing a big public performance at the tourist office on the lake, near the Prince Albert Museum.

The next morning they'd be driving me to Rae-Edzo, a mostly Aboriginal community where you were just as likely to find a forty-year-old mother of three in the Grade 10 classroom as you were to find a teenager. I was especially excited about this visit, and especially anxious about looking like some eccentric rich guy from Toronto.

I had realized when I got to Yellowknife that the group who brought me in thought "performance artist" meant juggler, or sword swallower, or maybe magician. When I told them I planned to build fifty Inukshuks out of egg rolls from the Jade Garden Chinese Restaurant on Franklin, they looked at me like I was crazy.

"Oh boy, Ben, I've got to go with the doctor. He wants me to talk with some other doctor, a specialist. They've got a thing they want to try. I'm going to call you back — stay in your room and I'll call you back."

I listened to the dial tone for a while and then I hung up. The bed had stopped squeaking in the room above, and outside someone was vomiting and coughing while a bunch of other people laughed and shouted. It was Friday night and the streets were teeming outside the bars, where everyone gathered to smoke. I lay on my back on the huge bed and watched the red lights from RCMP cars blink up from the street and onto the ceiling of my hotel room.

Yellowknife is built on solid rock. Everything that happens there happens above-ground: plumbing, school, love, crime, sports, and banking. Everywhere you go you are aware that you are on rock, unless you're out on the lake, in a houseboat. But even then, as winter comes, you have to make sure your houseboat is level or else it'll get frozen on an angle and all your guests will go tumbling into the corner of your living room. For eight months, everything will roll from one side of your home to the other. Your coffee will spill. Your handwriting will be crooked. Eventually rock will push its way through the floor of the houseboat, just like it pushes itself through the floors of all houses. Eventually rock will push its way through the floor of the Gold Range, of the Wild Cat Café, and of Sam's Monkey Tree.

In Yellowknife, you know you are part of the earth. Everywhere you go, the rock follows your feet. There's no escaping it.

The phone never rang again that night and no one answered the phone at my dad's place. I fell asleep as morning sunlight began to creep through the crack in the curtains.

141

PUT IT IN
YOUR HEAD
INSTEAD

On the east-west platform of the St. George Subway Station, I plunged my right index finger into my right ear. It was rush hour, and I was on my way to the Metro Reference Library after visiting with Jake.

Jake wasn't doing any better, and the doctors no longer spoke of improvement or of a time *when*. This was going to be it for Jake, a life in endless repeating waves, a new world every time he woke up in the morning, or in the middle of the night. He still looked like Jake, if a little scruffy. They said he dressed himself every morning, and that getting dressed was one of those intuitive memories that don't seem to disappear. He knew when his clothes started to smell bad, and he'd ask for some clean ones, even though they were in the same closet beside his bed that they were always in. When he passed his bathroom, he was reminded to shave, and to brush his teeth. He was still good at all that.

But when he joined the rest of them for breakfast in the cafeteria, where he was escorted each morning, he asked what he was eating and said he'd never tasted anything so good. It was scrambled eggs, always scrambled eggs, and brown toast. By lunchtime, he still remembered food, and though it was different food from breakfast, and more varied from day to day, he didn't seem quite as excited. At breakfast, it was as if he were discovering food for the first time, but not at lunch. And by dinner, he occasionally remembered some of the dishes.

"This is beef, isn't it?" he'd ask.

And his residence friend Carson, who Jake met for the first time every day, would say, "Yes, it's beef. Beef with gravy."

"It's a cow."

"That's right, Jake."

"What's a cow again? Moo or ruff?"

"Moo."

"Which one is moo?"

"The cow."

143

But my ear — I'd had a sharp pain in my ear for weeks now. It felt like a blister, or a needle. On the subway-station platform I plunged my finger deeper into my ear than I'd ever done before, and I felt something give, felt something budge a little in there.

I clamped down on the object with my fingernail and slowly extracted it from my ear. Coated in a golden-brown sludge was the seed of a whirlybird. At least, that's what we used to call them when we were kids — those little helicopter blades that came spinning down from trees. I flicked the sticky mass into a trash container and looked around to see if anyone had been watching.

Crammed onto the westbound rush-hour subway car, I couldn't solve The Case of the Whirlybird in My Ear. But on my walk home north along Christie Street, as I gazed down into the Pits, where the Jews and the Italians had kicked fascist ass nearly seventy years ago, it struck me. A few weeks earlier, when Denise had been about to leave on an open-ended trip to South America, we'd gone for some drinks downtown, then taken the subway up to her neighbourhood. We went for a walk in the ravine near her house. She had to leave for the airport at noon the next day, but we walked nearly the entire night, talking like we never had before. At some point, we found ourselves holding hands.

This was strange, because Denise had once been Jake's girlfriend. She'd stood by him as long as she could, but finally got sick of introducing herself every time she came to see him at the home where he'd been put. "You're the lady who visits me!" Jake would say when she walked into his room. But he never remembered her name, and never remembered that they'd been lovers. "You were here yesterday, weren't you?" he'd ask, even when she hadn't been there for months.

She always hugged him when she came to visit, and every time she hugged him he was being hugged by a woman for the first time in his life.

In the ravine, in the mist of the morning, our walking slowed and we held each other's hands tighter. I liked the smallness of her hand in mine, I liked its warmth. I liked each finger on Denise's hand, and ran the pad of my thumb over each fingernail. We turned to face each other and, for the first time, I actually saw her eyes. They were dark eyes, and small.

145

I was a guy who'd eaten one thousand dough-nuts, I was a guy who'd staggered around the front window of an art gallery for twenty-four hours, and I was a guy who'd built a sacred stone man out of egg rolls in the Arctic.

Did she know she was looking at such a guy?

Her eyes were sad, or maybe she was just tired. Of course she was tired. She'd been trying to tie up loose ends for weeks. We'd bumped into each other in the Annex the day before and she'd told me about her travel plans. I suggested we grab a drink on that last night, even though I knew it was pretty presumptuous. But she was the only other person alive on this planet who had once been close to Jake, and I wanted to spend some time with her. She said she had plans for some going-away drinks at the Green Room with a bunch of friends, but would slip out early and meet me.

By now our walking had slowed to nearly a halt. We found a large rock to sit on, and Denise leaned into me. We were still clutching each other's hands, and she pressed her head against my chest. I lay my head down sideways on hers, and breathed in the fragrance of her hair. Her hair was thick, and wavy, and dyed black. Our hands slid up each other's arms and soon we held each other. Around us, whirlybirds spun to the ground and into the small creek that ran past us.

All these things surprised me equally.

I was trembling a little, I could feel my body tremble, not because I was cold, but because I was nervous. I was nervous, and exhilarated, and filled with fear. If she would only cancel her trip, stay right here in Toronto, I would build her a house out of egg rolls. I immediately felt guilty about the thought, but it wasn't like Jake would know the difference. I would build her a two-storey house out of egg rolls. With an egg-roll verandah and an egg-roll patio.

I don't know how long we held on to each other, but eventually we drew back and examined each other's faces. I was thinking it was so strange that we had these two eyes right up near the top of us, and then a nose under that, a mouth below, and an ear around either corner. All these things that were about our senses were stuck onto our heads. We were like giant antennae. Giant antennae walking down the street, opening up bank accounts, buying

147

hamburgers and deciding what to put on them, falling in love with other giant antennae. That's what I was thinking when she took one of my hands, opened it on her lap, and turned it palm-up. With the very tip of her right index finger, she began tracing paths on my palm. I watched, wondering where she was trying to get to.

We peered silently into the creek, and from beyond the ravine, we heard the faint, steady hum of traffic on the 401, where trucks rumbled all night long, and there was the occasional barking of a dog. A bird fluttered in the branches above our heads. It was going to be time for Denise to go soon. She took off her watch and flung it into the creek. I took off my watch and did the same. We were pissed off at time.

She explained that she'd been a snowflake in an elementary-school play. I told her I'd been a zombie in my junior high's theatre festival. At some point the sun came up. At some point she turned her face up to mine and we kissed. At some point a whirly-bird sailed down from the trees above, directly towards my ear.

NERVE
ENDINGS

When I walked into Billy Billy Donuts at nearly three in the morning, I smelled like ketchup and my scalp felt like I had elastic bands clinging tight to my hairs. I had spent the evening at Porter + Haas, lying naked in a vat of ketchup, with only my head above the surface. I wore a pair of dark sunglasses and had a rectangle of tape over the bridge of my nose, and behind me a huge mural acted as a backdrop: a beach scene depicting the Atlantic Ocean stretching towards the horizon, seagulls swooping from fluffy white clouds, the handle of a red plastic shovel sticking out of the sand, and families standing knee-deep in the foamy water licking up onto the beach. In the sky, a biplane trailed a long white banner with the words "Nerve

Endings" printed across it. That was the name of this performance piece.

Coming out of speakers around the gallery space was a mix of bubble gum by Donovan, and Melanie, and the Turtles. I remained motionless in the ketchup. In fact, my eyes were closed behind the sunglasses. I had two electrodes adhered to my forehead. When viewers stepped forward to pull my hair, as various brightly hand-painted, carnival-style signs around the room urged them to do — "Pull the artist's hair! Everybody's doing it!" — the electrodes transmitted signals, through some kind of technology that I had to hire someone else to rig up, to a computer that instantly cut off the music, replacing it with a horrible human scream. Sometimes it was a man's scream, sometimes a woman's, and sometimes a child's. As soon as it ended, which it did abruptly, Donovan would come back on, singing about his shirt, or maybe Melanie singing about her roller skates.

I remember telling Denise about my plans for this exhibition a year earlier. She thought about it for a minute and said, "So you think people will keep pulling at your hair to drown out the awful Donovan music?"

Some people pulled and some people didn't. Occasionally I'd feel a hand reach out and just touch my hair gently, or maybe ruffle it a bit. I had no idea who was caressing and who was yanking. When someone stepped right up and pulled as hard as they could, there was only a dull pain at my scalp, perhaps because my hair was so thick that no individual strand had to take much stress.

I couldn't really justify the ketchup, but I thought it was a neat way to deal with the thousands of little packets I'd been collecting from Harvey's over the past few years. I always took a handful from their condiments bin. The day before the show, I'd invited about twenty people to Porter + Haas to rip open the packages and slowly fill the vat with the contents. The packages themselves were stuffed into a wire-mesh trash basket beside the tub and left there for the show. I had no idea what the point of this was: maybe the ketchup was supposed to represent blood. When Jake and I were kids and watched Westerns on TV on Saturday afternoons, he had told me, "Don't worry, it's not

151

real blood. It's just ketchup." So there I was, lying in a tub of B-movie blood. I'd let the gallery-goers make of it what they wanted.

And after everyone had left, and Brenda helped scrub me up in the gallery's little washroom, I still smelled like ketchup.

I smelled like ketchup and my head throbbed from all the hair-pulling.

So when I sat down beside Kim Novak in Billy Billy Donuts and ordered a chamomile tea and a raised chocolate, I was sure she could smell me, but I took comfort in knowing that I probably didn't smell as bad as her llamas.

"Your hair . . ." she said as she reached across the little square table towards my head. "It's sticking out all over the place. You look like Einstein or Beethoven. Or like Mischa Auer!"

Mischa Auer was an old character actor Kim Novak and I both liked. He had a thick Russian accent and always played whacky sidekicks in movies from the 1930s and live TV shows in the 1950s. Some of his most famous films were *My Man Godfrey*, *You Can't Take It with You*, and *Destry Rides Again*, which was maybe James

Stewart's best movie, plus Marlene Dietrich played Frenchy in that one. Mischa Auer's hair usually stuck out like he was a crazy man. He looked like a third-rate performance artist who'd just spent six hours in a bathtub full of ketchup while people tried to pull his hair out.

"All these people were pulling my hair," I explained to Kim. "It made Donovan stop singing, but it replaced that with a bunch of screams."

Kim smiled, and it reminded me of the way she smiled when she was drunk in *Pal Joey* and she said, "Confidentially, I'm stacked." She stroked my hair for just a second and I knew that I'd always remember the night that Kim Novak stroked my hair. She brought her fingertips to her nose and said quietly, "Ketchup."

"Right, ketchup. I was lying in a big vat of it so only my head was sticking out. I have no idea why. It just seemed like the right thing to do."

A small metal pot of tea was placed in front of me, and then an empty white cup and a napkin with a raised-chocolate doughnut on it.

"I used to go to school just a few blocks away from here," I told Kim as I poured tea into my cup. "I did all this insane performance stuff and they actually gave me credits for it. So I haven't stopped, though I don't get credits anymore. I get grants sometimes, but even those seem to have dried up since the Yellowknife egg-roll project." Then, seeing my tea was barely yellow, I poured it back into the metal pot.

"You need to let it steep for a while," Kim said. "That's a very strange word, isn't it? Steep."

In the far corner of the doughnut shop, a stocky, bearded man in a turban was talking on the pay-phone. "It smells like ketchup in here!" he said into the receiver. But really, I couldn't hear him from where I was. It's equally possible he said, "I really liked her in *The Notorious Landlady*!" Or maybe, "I wish they wouldn't have painted the concrete surface!" Or maybe, "I can't come home, because I don't remember where we live!"

Kim Novak was wearing a pair of black pants and a blue denim jacket over a lavender T-shirt. The only jewellery she had on was a modest wedding ring, and her makeup was limited to a couple of slashes of pale red lipstick and a hint of black eyeliner. She lifted her teacup and took a sip, then put it down again and looked right at me.

"You cry every time you see me fall out the bell-tower window, don't you, Ben?"

"It's always a surprise," I told her. "I always think it's not going to happen this time, that this time he's not going to be such an asshole." I filled up my cup again, and this time the hot water was yellow with chamomile. I took a couple of quick gulps and put the cup back down. "The first time I saw that movie, I was with my mom. Jake and my dad were off fishing for the weekend. I liked watching movies with my mom. All those movies with Deborah Kerr, and Barbara Stanwyck, and Lauren Bacall, and you."

"They were good, those three. They could really act."

Over in the corner, the bearded man began pounding the side of his fist against the telephone. The tall plant beside him rocked a little. The girl behind the counter shouted something I couldn't quite catch.

I looked back at Kim. "My mother had a real sense of justice. She couldn't believe that James

Stewart, of all people, could be such a prick.
I mean, that was part of what was so shocking.
James *Stewart*. But she told me that these people
had played with his mind so much that he didn't
know what he was doing anymore. He couldn't
control his emotions."

"Well, he was in love, too. And he couldn't
believe that she loved him, because he hated himself so much. That's the way I see it, anyway. But I
hate watching that movie. It's a good movie, but I
hate watching it."

156 I pushed a chunk of the doughnut into my
mouth and chewed it quickly. "My mom pointed
the gun right at him, and then there was a huge
bang, and he just collapsed onto the pavement. It's
hard to believe when your own mother does something like that. She was so calm about it, though,
so quiet and matter-of-fact. The way she saw it, he
had killed her whole family — all her aunts and
uncles, and maybe even some little cousins."

Kim Novak put her hand on mine and gave me
a light squeeze.

The girl behind the counter brought a tray of fresh crullers out from the back room and slid them onto a display rack.

The bearded man laughed suddenly and loudly, hung up the phone, shoved another quarter into the slot, and lifted the receiver again.

The coffeemaker spluttered and a little light on it changed from red to green.

Outside on the sidewalk, a dachshund appeared. He stopped suddenly right in front of the doughnut shop, his thick little body quivering.

IN THE
BACK OF THE
AMBULANCE

I knew that my father was sick, but I didn't know how sick he was. He had devoted himself to my mother for years while she was sick, and then after Jake got sick, my father devoted himself to Jake. Amid all this devoting of himself to other people, my father was starting to get eaten up by cancer.

I found this out far too late, maybe because I was willfully ignoring all the evidence. I'd come over and a teapot was smashed on the kitchen floor and he hadn't cleaned it up. "I was going to do it later," he'd say. "Don't worry about it."

"When did it happen, Dad?"

"This morning. Or maybe it was yesterday. It was after the cleaning lady was here."

So I'd unwrap the pastrami and rye bread I'd brought from the Pickle Barrel. This was his favourite thing: pastrami sandwiches. "Make me just a little one," he'd say, "but lots of mustard."

At the table, his fingers were restless. He was dying for a cigarette. He was pretending he no longer smoked, because he knew it would make me angry if he did, but the place smelled of smoke and some aerosol air freshener he thought would mask the evidence.

I knew he smoked, and he knew that I knew, but he still played the game of pretending he didn't smoke.

The pastrami sandwich in front of him, along with a glass half-filled with Coke and ice cubes, Dad said, "It's too bad Jake can't be here. Jake loves pastrami." I could tell he felt guilt with each bite he took. He would never forgive himself for that moment beyond his control on the boat.

He made his way through only half the sandwich before he pushed the plate away. "I'm going back to the bedroom. Thanks for bringing lunch."

That would be the end of conversation for the visit. He lay in his bed with his head propped up. I sat on the end of the bed, cross-legged. With the

TV on in front of us, he stared off into the distance, beyond the TV, beyond the wall, and beyond the wall beyond that. "You really like these Chuck Norris movies?" I asked.

There was silence for a while, and then he said, "What? Oh, yeah."

I only realized much later that he'd already been preparing himself. He'd put on his coat and hat and was inching towards the door. He no longer felt social. There was nothing he could add to what he'd done. He missed Mom.

They strapped Dad into the ambulance, and I climbed in beside him. He looked like he was really concentrating, or maybe it was the pain. My father had agreed to go to the hospital so long as they didn't turn on the siren or speed through the streets. He hated the idea of so much fuss, of all the attention it would draw. He hated being the centre of things. I had made them promise not to turn on the siren and not to speed through the streets. They agreed: it wouldn't make any difference anyway.

This was the first time I'd been in an ambulance, and the first time my dad had been in an ambulance. Neither of us liked it very much. It was no lobby of the Place Bonaventure Hotel. I sat on a bench opposite his gurney and placed my hand lightly on his forearm. He was strapped in and I could tell he was uncomfortable.

"We're going to get you back on your feet, Dad," I said.

The ambulance pulled out of the driveway of my father's house and onto the street, and Dad lifted his head a little to peer out the back window, the tiny square of back window. As we drove through the streets that had been his world for so many years, he said:

"That park — I used to play baseball in that park. There was a big fight once between all the Jewish kids and the kids who thought Hitler was a hero. The Italian boys helped us. We chased those Swastika kids down the back alleys, swinging our baseball bats.

"That apartment building is where Harvey Lepofsky used to live, back before we were in business together. He was a real joker, Harvey, but

161

his wife never laughed at his jokes. She just rolled her eyes.

"You had your bar mitzvah in that *shul*, didn't you? I fell down dancing with your mother — two drinks was all it took. Uncle Sully died the next day in Winnipeg.

"My office was right up there, before the fire. Remember that fire? We went in after and sifted through the ashes, looking for important papers and your mother's ring, which I kept on my desk, but the firemen kicked us out. We smelled like soot for weeks."

He couldn't possibly see anything through that window but telephone wires and traffic lights, but he got all the landmarks right. I stroked his shoulders, his thin shoulders, gently.

And he lay his head back and named all the streets we passed, and those with no name, he gave them names.

It was the last thing my father did.

I AM
A BULLET

What was the bullet thinking, I often wonder, as it raced towards the thick, ugly, cobwebbed skull of Rolf Köber? And what could it see during its lightning trajectory? Was Rolf Köber all skull to the bullet, or all brain? A skull to be shattered like a bowling ball scatters pins? A brain to be burrowed deep into, like a worm through soil?

Maybe that's the kind of thing that bullets think. Did the bullet think, *I'm going to kill that fucking piece of self-satisfied Nazi scum. That hateful wisp of near-human detritus. I'm going to inflict pain on him like he's never felt before, but just one searing burst before his life vanishes from the face of the earth like a tiny red ant being flicked off a forearm. And then his wife will feel pain, and his children will feel pain, and eventually they will wonder how they ever could have lived in the same house as such a seething, stinking pile of evil, such a smudge of pus on the earth's surface.*

Maybe that's the kind of thing that bullets think.

Perhaps the bullet thought, *Hey, this is cool! I'm flying! Look, Ma — no hands! Yee-ha!*

Maybe that's how bullets think.

So far as I am aware, studies haven't been done on how bullets think, so it's tough to know for certain about the thought processes of these compact high-velocity lethal projectiles.

I opened the door of my cluttered storage closet and pushed aside cartons of books that wouldn't fit on my shelves and garbage bags filled with old clothes. Some of the clothes were mine, and some had belonged to my father. I think there was a suit of Jake's in there somewhere, too. It was unlikely he'd ever need a suit again.

A couple of layers in, I came to a stack of plastic milk crates crammed with old issues of *Rolling Stone*, their covers ripped where rusting staples held them together. There were also copies of *Creem* and *Trouser Press*, and the yellowing, frayed newsprint of *New Musical Express*.

NME.

Rolf Köber was my NME. He was the only NME I'd ever had. He was the NME of everything that was good, everything that had once been good, on this earth and in my life. He was the NME of the Buzzcocks, of the Fabulous Poodles, of Kate Bush, Graham Parker, the Slits, the Piranhas, Red Krayola, the Soft Boys, Pere Ubu, the Jam, Blondie, Richard Hell and the Voidoids, Captain Sensible.

Rolf Köber was the NME of the Clash and of Johnny Cash. Of Leonard Cohen.

He was the NME of Warren Zevon, of were-wolves of London, of lawyers, guns, and money, of Mohammed's radio.

The enemy of Television and Talking Heads.

Rolf Köber was the enemy of Bob Dylan circa *Street-Legal*, but also *Planet Waves* and *Self-Portrait*, of the first Trio album, of Nick Lowe, David Bowie's *Low*, Elvis Costello, Wreckless Eric, Dusty Springfield, Randy Newman, and Ian Dury and the Blockheads' *New Boots and Panties!!* He was the enemy of Joan Armatrading, and Roy

165

Orbison, and the Original Five Blind Boys of Mississippi. Martin Hum and the Hummingbirds, the Dixie Hummingbirds, the Swan Silvertones, the Sensational Nightingales, the Famous Blue Jay Singers, the Flamingos, and the Falcons' "You're So Fine." Sam Cooke, with and without the Soul Stirrers, running naked down the hallway of a motel where'd he'd rented a three-dollar room.

"Jesus Hits Like the Atom Bomb," "Is She Really Going Out With Him?," "You'll Always Find Me in the Kitchen at Parties," "Strange Man, Changed Man," "(I'm Always Touched by Your) Presence, Dear," "Touch the Hem of His Garment," "C-30! C-60! C-90! Go!," "Romance Without Finance Is a Nuisance," "The Man Who Couldn't Afford to Orgy," the Bangles' "Eternal Flame," and "Yeh Yeh," by Georgie Fame and the Blue Flames.

Rolf Köber was the enemy of Iggy Pop's "The Passenger." And of Michelangelo Antonioni's *The Passenger.* Of *The Double Life of Veronique, Vertigo, The Blue Angel, We're No Angels, The Desperate Hours, Despair, A Place in the Sun, A Raisin in the Sun, Closely Watched Trains,*

Strangers on a Train, *Paris*, *Texas*, and *The Texas Chain Saw Massacre*.

He was the enemy of Werner Herzog and Wim Wenders, and of Preston Sturges, Terrence Malick, Pier Paolo Pasolini, and Alejandro Jodorowsky. Of Orson Welles and Charles Laughton. Robin Wood and Woody Allen.

He was the enemy of Vito Acconci, Yoko Ono, Andy Warhol, Laurie Anderson, and Gilbert and George. Of Joan Jonas, the Kipper Kids, Allan Kaprow, Hugo Ball, Carolee Schneemann, and Tristan Tzara. Of Greg Curnoe, Barbara Caruso, and Joe Brainard.

Rolf Köber was the enemy of Art Tatum, Art Pepper, Art Carney, Jackie Gleason, Jackie Mason, and Jackie McLean. And *Get Smart!*

He was the enemy of Frank O'Hara, Wisława Szymborska, Blaise Cendrars, bpNichol, and Salvatore Quasimodo.

He was the enemy of Samuel Beckett.

When that bullet hurtled towards Rolf Köber's skull, on the sidewalk of a strip mall in Bathurst Manor Plaza, in front of Faggot's Hardware, in

September 1990, was it thinking, *I am going to kill the enemy of Samuel Beckett*?

Maybe that's how bullets think.

I dug out my sack of toys from when I was a kid and dragged it through the path I'd cleared into the hallway. The biggest thing in there was the Johnny Seven. The Johnny Seven featured seven ways to kill. I pulled on the night-vision goggles, which were snug around my adult head, and dropped myself in the green wing chair in my living room. The chair was worn now, decades old, but for the first time I noticed the swirling floral patterns sewn into its surface. Green thread on green fabric. Strangely shiny. I wedged the butt of the rifle between my knees and pressed my forehead against Johnny Seven's powerful barrel. Its cool brown plastic felt natural and correct against my brow.

I asked the bullet what it was thinking. The bullet said nothing. The bullet was aware of the value of mystery.

When I pulled the trigger of my Johnny Seven, pulled it down with my thumb, the gun jumped, as if I'd frightened it. It fell from between my knees and I slumped forward in the wing chair.

This wing chair had cradled my mother as cancer gnawed at her body, and my father, too, as cancer had gnawed at his, though in a much less public way. My mother and father liked to sit in this wing chair and read the newspaper. My father would sit there while my mother cooked roast beef and potatoes, with maybe a side plate of farfel. My mother sat there while my father planed down the bottom of a door so it would close properly, or while he built a brick barbecue in the backyard.

Both read the front section of the newspaper, and my father read Sports. My mother read Family, formerly titled Women's, and my father glanced at Business. My mother read Travel, and my father leafed distractedly through Wheels. My mother always read the obituaries, and it always seemed like someone's aunt, or father, or niece, or cousin — named Leibowitz, or Farber, or Fishbaum, or Blatt, or Gould, or Razovsky — was dying. And then my father would put on a suit, and before he went into work that day, he would drive to a funeral home somewhere in Toronto, or just

169

north of Toronto, or occasionally Hamilton, and he would say goodbye, sometimes to people he'd never even met.

Sometimes, at the funeral home, he'd be handed a pair of black gloves and would perform that most meaningful of mitzvahs — carrying the coffin to the hearse, and then from the hearse to the plot: the favour that can never be returned. He'd stand around the open grave amid the family and friends of the dead, and watch the coffin sink slowly down on a hydraulic lift, and though he couldn't read Hebrew, he knew most of the words to the mourner's kaddish, and he knew when to say Amen, though we pronounced it "ahmeyn." When it was his turn, he picked up the shovel, stabbed it into the heap of dirt beside the grave, and tossed a clump down onto the coffin. He hated doing that — throwing dirt onto the dead — but it was tradition, and so he did it. I liked the idea: it was like tucking someone into bed for the final time, and doing it communally.

When our parents weren't reading the newspaper, Jake and I used to crawl all over this green wing chair. It was another universe, a distant planet, a jungle, a mountain, a warship, a statue, a skyscraper.

Jake remembered things then. That was when he remembered things. He remembered the last time we'd played and who'd got to be the good guy and who the bad guy. He remembered the names of Illya Kuryakin and Napoleon Solo. He remembered my name, too. He used to remember my name every time.

He remembered where we lived before Pannahill, though I didn't, because I hadn't been born yet then. He remembered how to put on his clothes, make a peanut butter sandwich, move the pieces on a chessboard, and dial a phone. He remembered our grandmother, who I'd never met, who was a sad woman, she always looked sad in the pictures Mom showed me, who spent her last two decades, nearly half her life, mourning for her brothers and sisters, and uncles and aunts who had disappeared into the black-and-white abyss of occupied Poland, each clutching a small bag, a treasured family trinket, official papers.

My vision was blurring as I gazed through my night-vision goggles at the Johnny Seven that lay on the scratched hardwood floor between my feet. My head felt light, and then it felt heavy, and then it felt light.

I could hear the torrents of blood rushing through my head, like the sound of an ocean in a seashell. I remembered an educational film I'd seen every year in grade school: *Hemo the Magnificent*. I used to hide my eyes during that one, because I couldn't stand to look at a beating heart.

There were guts inside me, I'd seen pictures of them in the 1966 *World Book Encyclopedia*, all these guts wrapped around bones. My white skull clutched tight to the big grey blob of my brain, but not so tight that it hurt. Veins and arteries snaked all over inside me, there'd been diagrams of them, too, slithering along my arms and legs, reaching right into my fingers and toes, hissing at intruders.

Stripped of our skin, we were pretty weird-looking, we people.

If I moved my legs, I could stand and walk, or even run, or stomp on a silverfish. If I moved my arms, I could wave, conduct a small band, throw a baseball, pull myself up onto a rotting wooden dock, make a tomato sandwich.

If I didn't move, if I chose never to move again, then I'd be dead. Being dead is when you just stop moving. You feel your body and your limbs, but you keep putting off moving them, keep putting off moving them, keep putting off moving them.

I sat there, slumped in the green wing chair with the floral patterns I'd only just noticed, and thought about if I should move.

SWIMMING

Fluorescent light pours out the windowfront of the doughnut shop, and I stand in the rectangle of its glow. It doesn't make me any warmer on this cool night, snow drifting like confetti along the sidewalk. My hands are deep in my jacket pockets, where I buried them nearly half an hour ago.

The street has been empty all this time, and suddenly it is not. An ambulance passes slowly in front of me. It is silent. Its red light doesn't flash and its headlights are off. I peer into the windshield. In the dark, it looks like no one is driving. When the ambulance turns the corner at the end of the block, and the street is once again empty, I can't convince myself that I actually saw it.

Across the road, in the darkened doorway of a closed shoe store, a man in shorts and boxing gloves dances from foot to foot, jabbing into the air in front of him. Ducking, then jabbing, his torso swivelling like he's a dancer. He puffs loudly through puckered lips, wipes his brow with the back of a glove. I see his breath. He's been through so much, and not only in the ring. His life has not been an easy one.

Behind me, the lights in the doughnut shop are turned out. There's a different sort of silence now. I peer up, and the sky is dark blue, nearly black. Clouds that look like wisps of backlit crepe paper shuffle by. There are no stars up there, no sign of the moon.

Soon I hear the distant roar of a plane, but can't see it anywhere. I do, however, see me, or someone who looks a lot like me, swimming through the night sky. He swims slowly, with steady strokes, heading north.

ACKNOWLEDGEMENTS

Many friends read the manuscript for this novel at various stages, and I am grateful to all of them. Thank you, Heather, Michelle, Gary. Thanks, Laurie. Thank you, Jack David and Michael Holmes at ECW Press, and copy editor Emily Schultz. Thanks, brother Barry.

This novel was written with the vital support of the Canada Council for the Arts, the Ontario Arts Council, and the Toronto Arts Council. Thanks once again to Terry Taylor for writing time in the magical cabin. Thanks to Carolyn Smart and the Department of English at Queen's University, where I wrestled with the final edits during my fall 2010 residency.

Finally, thanks to those who have hosted my readings and workshops, those who have bought my books, and those who have read them.

ABOUT THE AUTHOR

Stuart Ross grew up in Bathurst Manor. He published his first tiny collection of poems on the photocopier in his dad's office in 1979, and went on to sell over 7,000 copies of his chapbooks on the streets of Toronto. Stuart is co-founder of the Toronto Small Press Book Fair, a founding member of the Meet the Presses collective, fiction and poetry editor at *This Magazine*, and editor of his own imprint at Mansfield Press. In addition to scores of chapbooks, he is the author of two collaborative novels, a collection of essays, six books of poetry, and two short-story collections — the most recent, *Buying Cigarettes for the Dog*, won the 2010 ReLit Award for Short Fiction. Stuart has taught writing workshops across the country and was the 2010 Writer-in-Residence at Queen's University. A Toronto fixture for nearly fifty years, Stuart now lives in Cobourg, Ontario.

metonomy- the literal term
has been replaced w/
something w/ close meaning
b/c of a common experience
(Hollywood for film, suits for
 business)
synectache- part symbolizes
whole
"hired hands" for football
"wheels" for car

$M = []$

in tense

Jake- enviable to
Ben, every day
is new (exciting)
while Ben is laid
down

performing his
constraint

end of the movie, end
of the war - can watch
it, can't stop it